THE ESSENCE OF THE WITCH ROSE

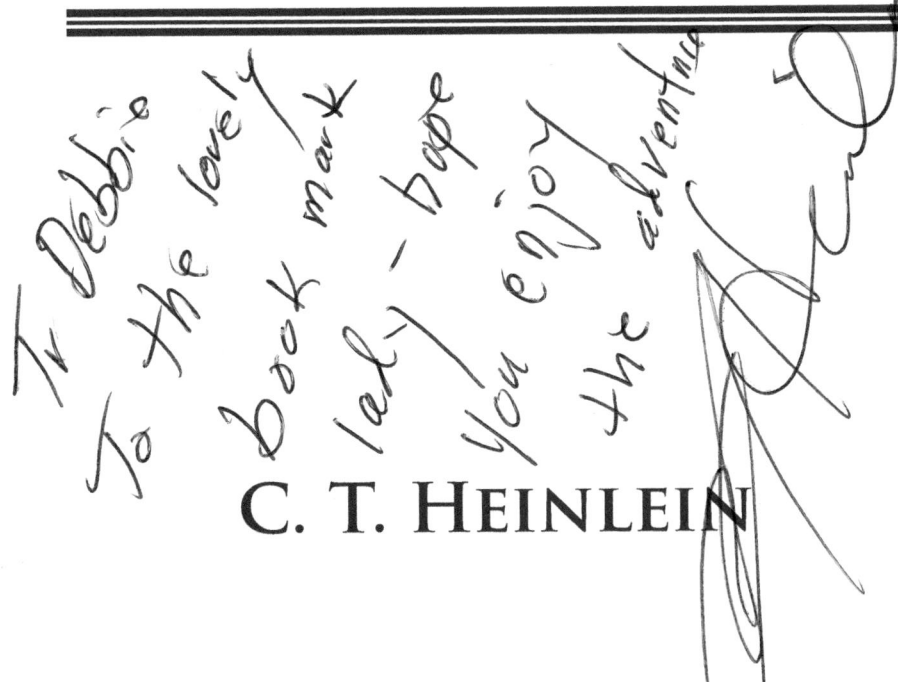

C. T. HEINLEIN

To Debbie
To the lovely
book mark
lady — hope
you enjoy
the adventure

PAGE PUBLISHING
Conneaut Lake, PA

First originally published by Page Publishing 2021

ISBN 978-1-6624-6157-6 (pbk)
ISBN 978-1-6624-6158-3 (digital)

Printed in the United States of America

To Jody Lyn, the starlight of my life

I t was always a rain like this that brought back my last memory of Salem's face. It had been coming down nail-hammering hard then as well. Only, unlike today, on that evening, the summer warmth was never allowed a chance to fuse into the rain.

It was the cold soaking rain that dragged a silver twist of silver hair down from the forehead and across Salem's face.

It was almost a warped divider forming two ragged halves. First of all, tracing a pathway between Salem's eyebrow, only to jump to the other side for an end, run around down the length of her nose. Once it reached the end nose, it tangled back to form a narrow mustache under her nose and back down on the far side of her mouth to end in a dagger-point tip, just short of her jawline.

And it wasn't alone.

There was a multitude of companion strands coming together to frame Salem's face and head, like a silver helmet from the time of the ancient Norse, back when the Valkyries swept over the battlefield looking for heroes for their heavenly rewards in Valhalla.

But it was the twisted strands in front I remembered most.

That and the look in her devilish cat-shaped green eyes.

They seemed to contain relief, a sense of loss, and something more I could not place.

All at the same time.

It was the last of those emotions that seemed to haunt me the most.

But only during the summer rains when I parked outside my house and thought back, or perhaps at times during my sleep.

Splashing from my Ranger to the house in the last remnants of daylong rain, I let my mind drift off in a related tangent to the same memory.

CHAPTER ONE

You see, I am not a cat person.

I don't have anything against them.

But the last thing I needed in my life was a moist nose bumping my forehead pre-alarm. In my mind, that rode the irritation train right up there with finding a dead mouse squeezing up between my toes first thing in the morning.

Tripping over them as I came out of the bathroom was also not exactly their best selling point either. But it ran more in the middle range of the ruin-my-day happenings. You know, more like the ever-popular changing of the kitty litter or the fun chore of getting someone to feed them if you happen to do some travel.

At least with dogs you could just shove them in to the back seat, roll a window partway down, and take them along for the ride. Usually dogs rode in a truck better than most kids. Not as much fun, but quieter and less likely to need a sudden rest stop five minutes after you had just filled up with gas.

Still all in all, I liked kids better then cats or dogs, especially my grandchildren. Taylor, in some ways, more than the others.

After losing her father in Iraq, I had never expected to find her. When she finally did come into my life over six years later, she was the blessing I never thought to get.

A hard-earned blessing.

We had spent a lifetime one evening on a mountainside, fighting over her soul with Father, the leader of a coven or cult, whichever you cared to call it. I doubt if either of us would have survived without a lot of supernatural help from Junior, my deceased son.

7

I know most people would have considered my story a bad dream that never really happened. But most people have never faced a total evil, with nobody there to physically help.

If they had been, how would they have explained how a modern two-headed ax had converted itself into an ancient war ax with runes on it and everything? And it didn't just kill Father and his cult members; it sent them sparkling away into an empty nothing.

Yeah, I know, it sounds like I am crazy.

But believe me or not, it brought the youngest of my grand-daughters into my life. And at this very moment, Taylor was staying in my home for the coming school year.

Her mom and stepdad were finishing the last six months of John's tour of duty, and until last week, Taylor had spent the summer with them.

I figured this time Taylor might want to stay with them, but nope. Her plan of staying with Grandpa for her sophomore year of high school hadn't changed.

I had done my grandfatherly duty and encouraged Taylor to stay with her parents, but established grades and maintaining contact with her friends in class and sports won out.

And I was not the least unhappy about it.

Until today.

CHAPTER TWO

Like I said before.

Taylor and I had a special relationship forged on a Pennsylvania mountainside, by a combination of wind, rocky earth, rain, and lots of lightning.

But even with our special relationship, Taylor was still a teenager.

And as we all know; teenagers have their own unique way of getting on your nerves if you are an adult.

Lastly, I was a grandfather in my sixties—meaning I quantified by age, if not maturity as an adult.

Today, the rain had already dampened my day.

It had given me a morning spent running in and out of various places of business with the water splashing into the lower part of my jeans and soaking my socks. By the time I got home, I had a serious case of squeaking feet.

I figured the completion of morning errands earned me a hot shower and late lunch of soup or burgers and fries, depending on what my granddaughter had decided to fix.

Boy, was I wrong on all points!

As I stomped into my house, I found the kitchen empty of human company.

Worse yet, there was nothing cooking on the stove.

Glancing around the kitchen, I couldn't even find the makings for a cold lunch or something to shove into the microwave.

It wasn't like Taylor to volunteer a prepared lunch and then skip out on me, but Taylor was still a teenager. So with a shrug of resignation, I figured eating could wait until after the hot shower.

After all, what could go wrong with a shower?

You just walked in the bathroom, turned on the shower, stripped, and jumped in.

Easy enough.

The bathroom was located between my room and the kitchen.

Only I have heard some people even take their preparations a step further. They like to have a dry towel waiting at the end of the soaking, and I know this because I am one of those people.

But today all I found was both an empty towel rack and a cupboard in the same condition.

Oh, there were hand towels, but it took a crap load of them to dry off a full-size body.

Checking the laundry might help with a dry towel or two but still leave the mystery of the missing bathroom stash. My washing machine was not that big, and I had just done a load of towels and whites the day before. Counting this morning usage, maybe three towels could have been used. That was counting my one towel and Taylor's pair; she used a second one for turbaning her long blond hair for drying.

Unless Taylor had brought over the entire soccer team for a morning showering after practice, there should have been a cupboard full of clean bath towels.

I did a quick check of both the washing and drying levels of my stacker. I found nothing in the washer and just a fuzz ball I had missed coming out of the lint trap in the dryer.

I did a two-handed lean on the cupboard and counted to twenty. My recent encounter with rain outside had left a ten count out of the question. Such a short period of time might have led to some family bloodshed.

Considering my granddaughter's karate skills, I didn't want it to be mine.

"Taylor!"

I got the answer almost as an echo, but not from the direction I expected.

It should have come from either Taylor's upstairs bedroom or the dining room, but not from my bedroom just beyond the second bathroom door.

"Taylor?"

I pushed through the door without thinking and found the last thing I expected.

Most days that would have been the stack of towels sitting on my bed. Many of them were still folded to one side on the bed, but more than a couple were scattered on the floor next to the bed.

More surprising was Taylor having a visitor spread across my bed.

Ratcheting it up another degree, the visitor was nude.

And female.

Not sure if that was for the better or worse.

But at least my granddaughter, Taylor, was fully dressed in damp blue jean shorts and one of the equally damp Johnny Cash T-shirts she had dug out of a collection of Junior-left-behind clothes.

Finding Taylor with a naked boy might have shortened his life expectation and, at the very least, gotten Taylor locked away until her graduation from college.

Not sure how to handle it with a female, but that concern melted away when I caught sight of the visitor's hair color, the sight of which pushed the unexpected sight all the way into the stratosphere, thereby forcing me to run the complete gambit of concern, joy, confusion, and probably a lot of other things spinning through my mind.

In the end, it took Taylor's interdiction to snap me out of it.

"Grandpa!"

CHAPTER THREE

I held my palm out toward Taylor without taking my eyes off the bed. Gawking is beyond rude, but I couldn't help myself.

"Grandpa!" Taylor dived across the nude girl to both cover her friend and grab a towel. "She's naked, and you're staring!"

Of course I was, but not in a sexual way.

It should have been sexual. Even with her obvious loss of weight, the nude was still a feminine thing of beauty.

"Grandpa"—Taylor stuffed a pair of towels around our visitor—"get out of here until she gets dressed."

That should have done it, but my eyes met those of our naked guest and I couldn't look away. You see, her eyes held the same emotions I remembered from her mountainside gaze.

"Been eight years and a lot of miles from here." And in my mind, the last of the haze was dragged away, leaving the memory with the crystal clearness of a mere moment ago. Even knowing the memory was real, many a time it felt more like a late-night scary movie that I had become too involved in.

"Now, Grandpa."

"Why all the towels?"

Leave it to me to pick up on the least important detail of the moment. It even slowed down Taylor's ire.

"She's not that big, and you should have gotten her dry with just one or two."

"She came in her cat form."

"Why?" I plopped down at the end of the bed, still missing the point of Taylor's objecting. "Why not human form instead?"

"Easier to catch mice," Salem added her voice for the first time, one more like a purr than I remembered, but that didn't matter. It was her comment that added to the reality of the situation. "And walking down the road naked would have likely attracted more attention than my feline form."

"How?"

I suddenly switched everything back to Taylor, including my look.

"She scratched at the door."

"And you let her in?" I kept rattling along as if I knew what I was talking about. "She might have been a stray tom with fleas or something."

"Not with that silver-colored fur." Taylor tugged at the towels to get them in a better position for covering. "And I noticed, while drying her off, she didn't have the right equipment to be a tom."

"But this cannot be happening!"

"It is." Taylor gave up the towel arranging and set up to grab my leg just above the knee. "And underneath your grumpy old age, so do you."

My words had come out a lot harsher than I had meant. Not for what had happened on the mountainside of long ago. It was more for what I could see coming in the very near future.

While Taylor did not seem to realize what the whole picture encompassed, I knew if the night back then had been real, then Salem coming here might be because of a need for a second trip back up the mountainside.

I had been too old back then, and that had been eight long aging years ago.

"Now?"

Taylor's dropped her hand away from my knee, and for a moment, I thought of giving in. After all, Taylor was my karate girl, a link to Junior buried long ago in Arlington, and a superspecial little lady even if there hadn't been a family bond.

But instead I looked past Taylor and made contact with Salem's cat eyes.

Then without another word, I got up and left the room.

CHAPTER FOUR

I only went as far as the kitchen.

Once there, I hesitated with a yearning look at the door and thoughts of the safer path beckoning me. Perhaps thinking back, I should have followed the impulse, but I didn't.

Instead I scrounged around the kitchen, finding items in both the pantry and fridge to make into a decent meal. It became a problem more of the choosing than lack of, A dilemma I did not see getting any easier.

I did my best to focus on choices with Taylor and Salem in mind. But my mind hopped from this choice to that and off again on a completely different tangent.

In the end, my head was back in the fridge when Taylor joined me. At least enough to lean on the doorjamb between rooms and oversee my efforts. I perched there waiting for her suggestions but got none or even a word of reproach.

"Did you give her some cat food?"

"Salem?"

"Why not? She is a part-time cat."

"Grandpa!"

Great.

Nothing is cuter than the indignation of a teenager, especially when I was the cause. I tried to maintain a serious demeanor with Taylor but loved teasing her even more than breathing.

"If not"—I stepped away from the fridge to start a dishwashing in an attempt to temporarily avoid the task of food choice—"did you offer Salem some milk?"

"We're all out. Somebody was supposed to pick up some more milk this morning!" Taylor gathered a dish towel and joined me at the sink. "I tried tuna fish."

"Did it work?"

"At the time, Salem was still in cat form. I got a sniff out of her, but not much else. She wouldn't even take a bite from my fingers." Taylor scooped up the first of my washing effort, a fork from last night. She followed the fork with a glass and rubbed at it until even the moisture from the next washing had to be gone. After the tenth run at drying the glass, she slowed down and finally stopped. "Do we actually have any cat food?"

"Not that I know of." I took the glass out of Taylor's fingers in exchange for a plate left over from the same meal. "But I can pick some up, when I run down to Hemlock for the milk."

"I would like it better if you got me a great big steak."

"Cow or otherwise?"

The comment was half smart-assed and half lost in the moment, as Salem joined us at the sink. She searched for a place to put away the glass and fork, finding them almost at once as if she had always been a part of the family.

I had known this moment was coming since Salem had first opened her eyes in the bedroom. They were a shade of green, which might have been common among the local feline population, but the up-and-down slit dividing them definitely shouted Salem.

The eyes and hair color were the only obvious things carrying over into Salem's human form. As a cat, Salem was oversize, to say the least, but human-wise, Salem was slender like the branch of a willow tree.

With her recent travels, Salem was even more slender now than before. But I had to admit, from a visual point of view, I was not complaining about either state of being.

CHAPTER FIVE

It was surprising I noticed Salem's loss of weight.

I would have guessed my female twosome would have dragged something down from Taylor's room. You know, a baggy sweatshirt from CMU and shorts that would have laced in the front and hidden the drop.

But no, they had raided my closet for an outfit.

Or maybe Salem had done the raiding after Taylor had come out to join me. Considering the choice, I couldn't fault the call either way.

My light-violet dress shirt didn't actually cover all that much. At best, it only reached midthigh and, with half of her movements, even less.

Still, the look was sensual without being suggestive or outright sexual. It was more of an "I am comfortable and at home" look.

At least as long as she didn't have to reach up toward the upper parts of the cupboards. Then, and only momentary at that, it might have chased away some of my old-man years.

With the last of the silverware being escorted into its proper sections of the drawer, I released the wash water and turned my thoughts back to the original problem.

"We got some open tuna fish, should I assume you like it no better in human form." Getting a down-her-nose look from a lady shorter than you tends to make the point without the need of words. "Or some venison hamburger I had out for dinner."

A smile hinting back at a long-forgotten memory crossed Salem's face. "If not overcooked, that sounds great to me."

"I could leave your burger raw."

"I would not want to offend Taylor with my eating habits."

Taylor, but not me.

Showed you where the old man rated.

I dug out some turmeric to mix in the burger, thought better of it, and turned to Salem with the container in my hand for approval or disgust.

"I have been around long enough to enjoy most spices." Salem's purr hedged a tiny bit toward a hiss as she finished, but not enough to be noticed by most people, but I did. "At least as long as they are not mixed with tuna fish or milk."

I shallowed my tactless comeback and just went on cooking.

Mostly to put off the conversation coming, but once setting over the food, Taylor brought up the lead in talk, which had to come first.

"Salem, how did you get here in cat form?"

"Started out as me hitchhiking and bumming rides with folks showing Michigan plates." Salem used a long bite and chew to slow down the telling, but as always, it didn't work. My Taylor stayed patiently on point waiting. "Had to ditch my clothes just short of here when a male folk tried to get into my pants at the rest stop."

"And?"

"I have to wonder how he explained the scratches on his face to his wife." Salem's grin went shit-eating wide. "I don't think his story about a girl changing into a cat is going to fly either."

Taylor got a couple more stories out of Salem's trials getting here. I liked the one best how she got out of a police lockup by doing the same thing.

Up until that morning, I never thought about how hard it would be for a cat to steal clothes, especially from a store or dog-guarded backyard.

In the end, she had to stay a cat for some forty miles of fox-infested walking. I am not sure how she had stayed on track, but it might have been some sisterly connection with Taylor or an address I had left behind without knowing.

Salem never said.

Either way, it became time for the important question of the hour. I actually gathered up my loins, in the form of some tugs on my present-day jeans, and asked Salem.

"Why did you come?"

CHAPTER SIX

Salem stared at her last bite of burger as if she hadn't heard my question.

"It could have been cooked a little less."

"And you could have given me more notice of your visit."

"Could have, should have." Salem maintained her stare as if I weren't there—until, with the help of gravity, a bit of the burger eased away from the fork and dropped toward the plate. "But I didn't."

I wanted to repeat my first question but lamely gave a repeated "Give notice?"

"Among other things." The bite disappeared into an animallike maul that didn't have time to want to chew it. "A lot of other things."

I looked away from the face I didn't want to search to my granddaughter's instead. Not only was Taylor's more readable; her answers were safer—at least it was most of the time.

Today not so much.

"Salem might feel better in some type of leg coverings."

"She might." Taylor's voice came out flat, a very seldom occurrence with any teenager, especially my granddaughter. Even more out of place, her voice stayed that way when she questioned Salem, "Would you?"

Salem dipped her head floor-wise as she rose from the table with a "tucking my dress shirt between her leg" motion. If anything, it exposed Salem in another way.

"I've got some shorts and sweats with drawstrings to make up for the waist difference." Still flat-voiced, Taylor kept pushing on, "They should work."

I made a motion to gather the breakfast settings to my seat, figuring I would come back to my questioning with Salem's form of dress less distracting. But surprisingly, my granddaughter saw it differently.

"But first!"

This time, there were several active tones in Taylor's voice, and she added on a couple more as she continued.

"You didn't answer my grandfather's question."

Say what?

Did I hear my granddaughter taking my side in an interrogation, at least to one degree or another? I couldn't believe that would ever happen, at least not while I was within earshot.

"After I find some pants?"

"Now would be better."

Damn it!

Taylor was going to her softball catcher's voice, the one where she took charge of the infielders to make sure they were in the proper positioning for a good defense.

It must have caught Salem off guard as well, having always been the older one and in charge of their relationship. After a moment more of posing over the table just short of mouth dropping, Salem slipped back into her chair with the shirttail dropping.

"I am not very good at asking for help."

"None of us are." At least not when I was younger, before shoveling wet snow became such a challenge. "But there are times we have to."

"Even worse, if I might have to take orders"—Salem's face came up to meet my gaze—"been doing that for way too many centuries."

This was the closest I had ever seen Salem come to losing control. She was acting like a human. And since I figured Salem's add-on was about the Father, an evil cult leader without a single drop of father goodness, I could understand the feeling.

"You still need to answer my grandpa's question."

Salem kept her eyes on me, and I figured it was time for me to get back involved as well.

"The other things?"

With something hidden deep inside, Salem reached out to either side to gather in both our hands. Then with an exhale, two degrees beyond lung emptying, Salem broke down her self-built lock and reached out to us as friends and possible saviors.

"The Witch Rose is not dead."

CHAPTER SEVEN

"**Y**ou're lying!"

Salem's hand jerked away from me like a winning lotto ticket that had burst into flames and destroyed itself. She tried the same with Taylor, but my granddaughter's grip was stronger than mine and refused to break.

"I mean you're wrong!" I scrambled for a truth, any truth that didn't involve Salem being right. "You have to be!"

That didn't help all that much, but at least Salem left off trying to disengage herself from Taylor. But it did nothing to lessen the steam in the eyes that were meeting mine.

"I saw the vines darken and die." I reached back into my forever nightmare, searching its darkness for every terror-soaked memory. "The whole thing crumbled away to blackened dust."

"And you figured that was the end?"

"Didn't you?"

Salem's eyes dropped away, and she began using a fingertip to push a crumb of burger around her plate. It was almost like a kitten at slow-motion play, but I would have figured Salem had long since outgrown such a distraction.

Still it was only after the shard of meat slipped off the plate and had dropped off the table that Salem's eyes meant mine again.

"I knew better."

"You what?"

Again, there was something a lot less than friendship in my voice.

For way too long, I had considered Salem an ally of the Father, only changing my mind because of her help at the end. Not only had she helped me destroy the Father and his evil supernatural cult, but she was there a second time as well.

After our successful confrontation with the Father, I had been carrying my granddaughter down the mountainside when an overlooked cult member came out of nowhere. It would have been the end of us but for an oversize cat leaping out to save us.

Until today that had been my last sight of Salem.

And now!

"We destroyed the limbs and body, but not the heart."

"How do you know?"

"Salem has always known."

Taylor's other hand came forward to take a double grasp on Salem's, either in comfort or to prevent her escape; I am not sure if even Taylor knew which.

"Did you?"

"Yes." Salem's confession came low, but with a strength telling us it wasn't wrong in her eyes.

"How?"

"An internal connection of the soul!" Again, it was Taylor a step ahead, and while I considered such a bit of information, Taylor went on, "But it could not have been with the Father. He had no soul."

Salem's eyes added on an assurance to Taylor's declaration and a seminegative to my "The Witch Rose?" throw out. After a moment, she returned Taylor's two-handed grip and looked to me with some of the old strength coming back.

"I have belonged to Mother Earth for a long time." My first thought was to wonder how long; my second was bumped away at a ninety-degree tangent. "It is her connection with the Witch Rose which extends to me. Because of which, I have become the Witch Rose's guardian."

I wanted to ask more but was having trouble digesting the revelation. Twice I raised a hand to speak but had nothing to go with the motion.

Finally, after several moments, Salem picked up our talk. "And over time, I have learned a great many of Mother Earth's secrets."

"Like what?"

My voice was still loaded with harshness but shaded with a touch of old-time nosy as well.

"Mother Earth seldom gives up her own." Salem released her grip on Taylor and turned her gaze completely to me. "Especially those she has owned for a long time."

"The Witch Rose?"

"And me!"

"So"—I dragged up all my feelings from back before our adventure on the mountainside and let them out with the bitterness of a rotted apple—"you're evil."

CHAPTER EIGHT

The color in Taylor's face drained away, like water over a cliff. Even before the echo of my words could have bounced off the nearest wall, her complexion was paler than the wearer of my dress shirt.

For all too long, Taylor had carried the memory of Salem in the black and white of a little girl's mind. Remembered were the good times of ice cream cones and playtime shared as with a grown-up sister.

Dampened by the passing of time was the terror, the kidnapping on the mountainside, and then Salem carrying her up to the Father. I admit some of which was overshadowed by Salem's soon-to-follow stance against the same terrified villain.

And most of all, Salem's last catlike appearance on our trip back down the mountainside where she came out of nowhere to saved us both from the last of the Father's followers.

And now?

I was calling her evil.

And Salem's answer?

"I hope not."

Salem's eyes went to a spot over my shoulder and refused to meet mine no matter how hard I tried to find them. In the end, I gave her a long moment to gather herself.

Finally, Salem continued with what sounded like a hangman's tightness in her speech.

"But for far too long, I have worn the chain of Mother Nature's connection with the Witch Rose." Salem gulped down something almost too large for her throat before adding, "Under which I have done some unforgivable things."

I am not completely sure if it was me or Taylor who squeaked out the "And now?"

"The Witch Rose calls to me from beneath the ground with the hunger of the ancients."

Yeah, that didn't sound creepy at all. At least to me, Taylor, on the other hand, shrugged it off with, "Are you going to give in?"

"Not yet, the Witch Rose is too weak from the beating you gave it." Salem again tightened a grip on both mine and Taylor's hands. "Normally, it would take centuries for the Witch Rose to get strong enough to change the call into a command. And even as a child of Mother Earth, I will not live forever."

"Then why are you suddenly here?"

"Did you miss us that much?" I added on as more prayer than honest hope.

"I missed you two every day and every night"—Salem's eyes sought the depths of mine—"but not enough to journey here with the chance of endangering you."

There was an honesty in Salem's comments.

But unsaid by her.

"It's going to get worse."

CHAPTER NINE

I finish off the breakfast dishes while the ladies dug into a better-looking outfit, or at least one that was less distracting in public. They put together a Johnny Cash T-shirt with a pair of Taylor's sweatpants from soccer.

The outfit was less sexy than my dress shirt but still a look that Salem pulled off. After my peek in the bedroom, I am not sure I could see Salem looking ugly in anything. But at least with this one, we could talk without me dreading and wanting a revealing peek all at the same time.

Salem spoke first, picking up her story by adding a new set of facts.

"Normally, the Witch Rose grows super slowly, especially when its available meals are nothing more than an occasional insect crawling in the wrong hidey-hole or a blown-along plant seed doing the same"—Salem lifted the fingers off the table to wave them in time to the recital—"but with the right force-feeding, it would grow much faster. Then in a decade, maybe less, the Witch Rose would be able to command me back."

"Don't force-feed it."

That was easy enough. Everything solved and we could go back to normal, but like most simple things, my answer was not going to work.

"I never would"—Salem's fingers stopped waving as she moved away from her prepared telling—"but others are hearing the call."

"Others, meaning more than one?" Taylor beat my asking the same thing, by less than an eye blink, but she did let me add in the "How many?"

"There is no way for me to know." Salem's fingertips tapped on the tabletop before edging back into the waving rhythm. "Three different groups have come so far, and given time, I am sure more will show up."

While Taylor hesitated to digest the new facts, I drove forward with the most important factor, "Why should I care?"

"Because once strong enough, the Witch Rose will drag me back"—Salem's eyes fogged over with memories that I think she would have rather forgotten—"and then the destroying of the young will begin again."

Not a good thing, still.

"You helped the Witch Rose before."

"And might again." The fingers went clawlike and stiffened attack-mode hard. "But given the choice, I would rather die."

"Why?"

"I got to know Taylor too well." Salem took her right hand off the table and just barely held back from reaching out to my grand-daughter. "And then you."

Taylor was special, but life changing?

"The inner cat was always my stronger half." Salem's looked between me and Taylor. "Knowing you two changed that. Now I listen to my human half first."

Not something I heard every day.

At the moment, it made even letters from my old students telling me what I had meant to them take second place.

"Who are the three?"

"A group of Peagen from the old world, the misguided from the desert of the Middle East, and your own bastards from the plains."

Great!

Now Salem wanted to play fifty riddles.

She couldn't go with something as simple as the Father, although his choice of titles could not have been more misguided. Jack the Ripper would have made a better choice of parent.

The Father's only connection with parenthood was when my son's love reached from beyond the grave, when he helped rescue Taylor, destroy the Father, and put an end to the worst evil ever.

"And in time, there will be more." Salem's hands came off the table and folded into her lap. "The evil ones are always the easiest to call."

"Good they can kill each other off and make the world a better place to live in." My mind crashed back to the thought of the Father's hand on my granddaughter. "If not, can they be any worse than the Father?"

"Are you sure?"

"I don't have to be." I ignored my granddaughter's frown and continued, "Pennsylvania is a long way away."

"I crossed it as a cat."

"You knew where to look."

"Grandpa!"

Taylor's frown was not shrinking, and I was not getting any closer to a smile myself. So I gave myself one more downwind tact, "Why us? You couldn't find anyone closer?"

"None who would believe my story."

CHAPTER TEN

Later that evening, we pulled my twin daughters into the mess over a pizza at my table. Well, actually two. My daughters had yet to realize that pineapple does not belong on pizza. And despite my career nurse's warning about overdoing it, I made sure the second pizza was heavily loaded with extra meat.

The twins, Jody and Jess, had once upon a time been graced with blond hair, a lot like the mane now sported by Taylor. But Jody, my medical expert, had let hers drift toward a dirty blond with light-blond highlights, while Jess had used modern science to help her hair into a strawberry-blond look.

Either hair color, they both looked great.

Good thing, since both were in the public eye from time to time.

Jess worked at the local TV station, mostly as their news programmer. She went through the suggested stories to decide what they could squeeze in and what had to be held back for lack of time, even going a step further on rare occasions where the station needed someone to fill in live on the street.

Jody, on the other hand, had chosen the medical field, working her way up the nursing ladder. Until now, Jody was in charge of a full floor at a convalescent hospital, which included the handling of our less-than-intelligent public, even occasionally on other floors when needed.

Also, more than once, she had shown up on her sister's news as a spokesperson for the hospital. She made for a much more agreeable sight than the higher-up administrators.

Their success had gone well beyond what I could have handled. In spite of what people claimed, teaching seemed a lot less stressful to me.

Surprisingly, after a minimum degree of discussion, both twins agreed we should help. It was my involvement that caused some discord at our tabletop meeting.

"Why should you be the one to go?"

Jody made the comment, but only because she voiced it first. Jess's face told me she was in complete agreement. There was also no real support from Taylor either, which was to be expected.

Since I had already firmly rebuked Taylor's involvement from beyond the limits of Hemlock, Taylor chose to display her disapproval as a teen pout.

"For evil to prevail, all it takes is for good men to do nothing."

"Good men, yes!" Jess double-teamed me from behind a pizza slice showing way too much pineapple. "Good grandpas, not so much."

"I still mow my own lawn with a push mower."

And bitched about being exhausted afterward, as all my girls knew.

"Mowing grass is a lot different than climbing mountains." You too, Taylor. "That's for young people like me."

The look I gave my granddaughter said it all, but I had to add a dig for her complete switch of alliance, "Right, last time, this old man carried you down that mountainside."

"I was a baby back then."

"You're still my baby."

That claim went over like a load of lead ball bearings over the Niagara Falls.

Then to my surprise, I got some unexpected support from Salem.

"But still too young to go back up the mountainside." Salem gathered in Taylor's hands and gave her one deep eye-to-eye look. "This isn't like the movies where a young teen disobeys her elders and becomes the hero in the end."

Taylor steamed instead of agreeing, and before anything else could be said, she stomped off toward her room to sulk. Behind her, I turned to the others with a meek "Junior's genes."

"Sure, but I am thinking he got those same genes from his dad."

Both of my daughters gave Salem an agreeing nod.

It wasn't exactly easy being the only male in a five-person meeting. And I still had a final point to make against the odds.

"And you girls are staying behind as well."

"Sure thing."

"Never thought otherwise."

I hated it when they did that twin thing, answering as if joined at the hip and sharing one mind. But at least they were verbally agreeing with me.

"And you will keep Taylor under control."

Again, I got the twin thing, but this time, they exchanged eye contact with each other. And for a moment, it reminded me of the long-ago times when they exchanged such looks.

It usually came when they were planning something I would not approve of. But certainly they would have outgrown that behavior by now.

At least it seemed so.

"No problem, I will take some vacation time while you are gone." Jess started the first half, and Jody added on, "That way, Jess can keep Taylor with her at all times."

I had gotten those dual grins more than a few times in the past, usually with results not coming out exactly how I had expected, but what could I do other than take Taylor with me?

And that was not going to happen.

I just had to be glad my girls were not crazy enough to want to go along with Salem and me.

CHAPTER ELEVEN

We stayed in the same hotel as John and I had used on the long-ago trip to recuse Taylor. Only this time, Salem and I actually had a choice, with a pair of chain places just down the road. They had been built years after our visit and departure and still carried some shine of newness.

The hotels weren't the only changes.

There was also a fast-food strip between our inn and the new places down the street. It even included a pair of sit-down places, with a choice of tableside service, or "get your own" from various offering.

Even the in and out roads had multiplied from two to five, all of which were either built or improved since the absence of the Father and his followers. Their increase went along with the growth in tourist attractions, which, in my less worldly opinion, were not worth the time it took to detour away from the highway.

All these new improvements should have brightened up the city, but to me, it gave the town a painted-over blandness, even worse than the old blandness, which still held on in the residential parts of the town.

Driving through them, I couldn't see where the houses were in any worse condition than before. Yet at the same time, I didn't see any real upgrade either.

There were a few houses sporting siding and a new swing set or two in the backyards. One house had even added a built-in pool. But in our short drive through the town, I didn't spot a single new house either here in the town proper or on any of the new outskirts.

It was like visiting a town where the people were frozen in the last century and were now charging forward at the speed of an Alaskan glacier.

Even the inn's waitress was still the same.

Well, maybe she was a little older now. There were a few wisps of gray mixed in the brown mop bundled up under the required hairnet, and the facial wrinkles were a bit more ingrained.

But the attitude?

It hadn't changed.

We were greeted with a frozen grimace that would have peeled the smile off Pollyanna.

I thought of opting for McDonald's down the street, but Salem gathered in my arm and nudged me deeper into the café, until finally letting me claim a booth toward the very rear of the place.

A nice-enough setting out of sight from the road, but not the entrance or our waitress.

The wicked witch of the inn followed after us to slap down a pair of menus squarely between me and Salem. It had the look of a well-rehearsed move coming from years of serving the public.

"Didn't think you would ever come back!"

"Didn't think I would be missed." Salem's words came with a smile, but no warmth.

"Hard not to."

Ms. Crabby Face's voice dropped into a stage whisper, still loud enough for everyone in the place to hear. But what could I say? She probably had little, if any, practice at whispering in public. While behind the nearby kitchen doors, even the loudest stage whisper would have been swallowed by the racket of the cooking.

"When you consider we have had people asking about you almost every day for the last couple of months, especially your friends from the church."

"I would never call that type of trash friends."

Salem's voice didn't show much emotion beyond a slight tightness. Most people would have missed it or passed the tightness off as being impatience with our server.

But I knew better.

After our long drive out here, I was beginning to pick up on some hidden mood readers of my companion. The roll under of the fingertips was a dead giveaway to Salem's tension level. The motion being repeated over and over did not bode well for our waitress's immediate future.

"Well, they live in your church."

"Their church, they bought it from the bank," Salem snapped up the menu as if she was really going to read over breakfast offerings. "I moved out before they finished the purchase and moved in."

"Don't blame you there."

If anything, the waitress's frown soured another two degrees and had not been very sweet to begin with. But there was a sense of improvement.

The sourness was directed away from us, toward the strangers in the church.

"Anyone who would protest a soldier's funeral is sick, and have you seen those signs they carry?"

"I try not to." Her question directed to me was the first sign she recognized my existence. Only I could have hoped for a better subject. "My son was killed in Iraq."

CHAPTER TWELVE

I t almost seemed as if our waitress's face softened a bit. You know, as if she actually cared. But I doubt it, as her expression remained rock-hard as she turned dagger comments back toward Salem.

"Your group in the rental house is not much better."

You had to wonder if this lady hated everyone or just those people she could match up with Salem in one form or another, which brought up the question of where I stood with the waitress.

The way she talked, maybe eating here was not the best idea.

I, for one, did not care for the idea of having spit in my food.

But at least for now, Ms. Motor Mouth was preoccupied with her lecture on the second group of recent arrivals, the ones Salem claimed had come from the deserts of the Middle East and perhaps the most openly dangerous of the three groups.

"They are all men and only come in here to order tea and stink up the place." With a shift of weight to include me, she spat out the rest of her recital, "While they wait for you to show up and chase away our real customers."

Salem's finger went past the hard bending to a clawing. If she had been in her cat form, I am not sure the tabletop would have survived.

And if the verbal riding got much worse, I am not sure the waitress would survive. It surprised me now that Salem was able to keep it under control while answering.

"Not my rental."

"You stayed there for one very long time."

"I didn't seem to have many choices." Salem's voice was a lot steadier than her fingers. "Not a lot of people were coming forward to offer me a place to stay."

"Then why give it up and move to the church?"

"The state took the rental over for nonpayment of taxes." Salem didn't offer Father's lack of touchable income as an excuse, and I had to bite my tongue. Once started, I might have added a lot of previously unknown facts to the conversation.

And being truthful at the moment, it was not my business to protect Salem. If Salem couldn't handle the words of a soured-out waitress, we were in real trouble. I had a feeling the invaders surging into town after the Witch Rose were going to use things a lot rougher than words.

"Anyway, I don't like them." Our waitress finally put her pencil to the notepad as if she was actually going to take our order. "They look like a bunch of terrorists to me."

"Sounds like your little town is going to hell."

I shouldn't have broken in, but from what Salem had filled in about this group of visitors, our opinionated waitress was closer to the truth than she knew.

Taking in my comment about her town, our waitress's expression actually shifted. It went from shrewlike disapproval to overworked fatigue.

She pen-tapped the notepad a dozen times before reaching down to cover Salem's hand. By either luck or intention, the old lady picked the hand that Salem had been clawing the table with.

"That's why no one expected you to come back."

Salem forced out a smile that might have been half meant.

At the moment, it was hard to tell how Salem felt. From the look on her face, I half expected Salem to go cat on me and dash out the door.

Thankfully, she stayed human and offered up a half-lame excuse, "Unfinished business."

"Here or away?"

"Both."

Salem's words came out low and controlled.

The tired old lady standing beside our table actually held her tongue for a long count of twenty, perhaps hoping Salem would offer more, perhaps for once having no idea what to say.

Finally, with the slowness of the elderly, the waitress released Salem's hand. Continuing the movement on further, the old gal gathered up the menus and shoved the notepad and pen back into her apron pocket.

"I'll get you the special." The menus found a niche under the tired old lady's arm, and she added a qualifier, "Our regular cook is out sick, and his stand-in can only cook one thing worth eating."

I tried to grab the old lady's hand, at least long enough to find out what the special was.

But I never got the question out.

I could have asked, because the waitress did stop to look back. But the old crab I was expecting had swam away, only leaving behind a pair of old bleached-out blue eyes with a set of tears forming up into big drops ready to fall.

Only they didn't fall.

Instead, they froze in the eyes like blue diamonds. The worn-out sorrow on full display in her next words.

"Take care of both our girls. Even before our town went to hell, they were the only two in this place making it a little better to live in."

Chapter Thirteen

O kay.

Ms. Sourpuss's last comment had brought up a couple of questions. They probably weren't that important to the overall view of our situation, and I should have just let it slide, but there was something about the use of that one word that bothered me.

Whom did she mean by both?

Salem and Sandy, Sandy and Taylor, or Taylor and Salem—none of which made any sense. Since the only one here was Salem, or was there another young girl I knew nothing about?

But I didn't get a chance to ask my questions.

Shortly after our food's arrival, the café began filling up with a second wave of breakfast goers. Most of them Salem and I dismissed as harmless, locals, or inn guests too lazy to check out anything down the road. But there were two tables not so easy to ignore.

The first table in, just to the right of the door, held five younger-aged men, with the second table over holding four more. None of the nine came anywhere close to fitting either of my harmless descriptions.

Their entrance alone had been enough.

They had spent way too much study time looking over the tables toward the front. Better trained, they might have walked the full length of the room and checked out booths in the back. But they were lazy and thought door guarding would work just as well.

Their general looks pegged them as natives of the Persian Gulf area, with a selection of Afghan-Pakistani thrown in for good measure. Their clothes might have suggested they had been Westernized from an East Coast point of view, but I was from the Midwest.

Ordering some bacon, eggs, or even a few pancakes might have helped them blend in. But just drinking tea with a couple of dark coffees mixed in for the second table told me they did not belong here.

"Part of the misguided?"

Salem nodded while slipping just a tad deeper into the booth in an effort to keep her face out of sight.

"But as you can see, not the thinking part."

"And to think our government doesn't care."

"We're at peace with them, or so our government says."

I shut my mouth, knowing just how much either of us believed in that comment. Our present twenty-fifteen government had chosen all too many policies that we disagreed with.

But today my worries did go much beyond my booth.

While no doubt I could walk right on by the watchers without gathering any attention, the same could not be said for Salem with her silver-colored hair being an attention grabber. And if that did not confirm their success hunt, a close gaze into the shape of Salem's slanted irises would.

I checked out the men a second time.

They were creepy enough, but nothing compared to the Father. And in the end, Salem and I had handled him and his followers.

Not sure why, but I am sure we could do the same with a bunch of overgrown haters from the Middle East. Of course, Salem had called for help against three groups, and maybe the others were tougher-looking.

Either way, Salem has spent the better part of four months as a cat to avoid these men.

Not the easiest of feats.

Salem's trip might have been easier if she had stayed in young-girl mode. The rides would have probably been a lot easier to get, especially if she was forced to beg naked, with more out-of-the-way detours in her favor.

Not at all like the detour she had been forced to take to Kentucky. She had meowed the trip out of a small child, not realizing it was soon to be changed over to a southern drive.

But this group of out-of-place young men had forced Salem to develop a paranoid side. One bad enough to accept a minor delay over the chance of discovery.

I thought about contacting the police again, but without an official ID for Salem, they would have been more trouble than help. Using Salem's changing-form trick might have gotten their attention. But more than likely, a need for help would have become a quickie trip to some nearby lab for testing and maybe even a dissection.

Neither of those outcomes rated very high on the appealing list to Salem.

Or to me, for that matter.

At the moment, it seemed all I could do was sit here and study Salem's damn silver hair while hoping the Arabs stayed up in the front.

"We should have dyed your hair."

CHAPTER FOURTEEN

"We tried several times with dyes from every company in your local Meijers and a professional helper from your daughter's favorite salon."

Yep, we had, and each time after we were done, the dye bleached out Salem's flowing strands in beads that dropped away like the leaves of fall.

I even thought about suggesting a haircut but was afraid how that would work out. It might come back all at once, or since Salem claimed it had never been cut, it might not come back at all. And of course, there was the worst possible outcome. Maybe like Samson, her hair was the source of Salem's power to change.

And I really hated the idea of Salem becoming a forever cat.

Just for Taylor's sake, of course.

Since I myself was not emotionally involved in any way.

In the end, I figured changing Salem's looks would be about as easy as flying to the moon by flapping my arms while holding a couple of eagle feathers.

"You think the restrooms have windows?"

"Not unless they lead to a secret opening in the lobby."

"Good point."

Not one I wanted to hear, but a good point all the same.

I ran my remaining piece of rye toast around the plate searching for yolk. It gave me a chance to think about our present situation as I topped off the yolked-up bread. Then with a piece of added bacon on top, I took a bite off the closer end.

"We could just walk out the door and hope they don't notice."

Salem's look almost knocked the yolk off my toast.

"Or maybe they gave up looking for you by now and are here for the tea."

And the sky was really neon green with pink highlights.

Why couldn't they just go away and get run over by a fleet of trucks?

I know I would have been happy to stay away.

My adventure on the mountainside was eight years and a hundred degrees out of my comfort zone. If it hadn't been for the bull-headed attitude of my granddaughter, which was another family trait passed down by my son, I would have passed on this trip with a hard-hammered no.

But no matter what, for this trip, better me than Taylor.

I looked across the booth to where Salem was working on the last of her bacon. She was using nibbling bites a lot smaller than the ones she had used the week before to wolf down the food in my kitchen.

It was funny how a few days of rest and a large dose of my cooking had put a covering back on Salem's ribs. Now my companion in the booth had the human form that was a match for the lean and sleek body of the hunting cat of the night.

"You might be right, but do you remember the single-mindedness of the Father and his followers?" The last of Salem's bacon disappeared behind her pearl-like teeth, and she went on as if I had nodded a yes. "Do you really want to take the chance that these out-of-place desert cockroaches are any different?"

Not in the least.

But I also didn't see us sitting here all day.

Frist of all, we would not be getting much done.

Second of all, there was only so much we could order and eat. Eventually, either the café would need our table for the lunchtime rush, or one of the door guardians would get bored enough to check out the rear of the café.

And third of all, I hated being trapped.

It brought back the worst of my fears, and even thinking about it tightened my chest and chilled my spine.

So, maybe a bandanna?

We could wrap the bandanna around Salem's hair and hide it from the bad guys.

Of course I had no idea where to find a bandanna in this crowd, and if I did, the bandanna would have to be extra large to handle Salem's silver mop without some of the silver strands hanging out the side.

Besides, this was a hot August day and not the best weather for a bandanna, unless, of course, we could also find me a biker jacket and a Harley suddenly parked outside.

Flustered with the situation, I gave the last of my toast an evil stare. I didn't see any way my day could have gotten any worse. So in frustration, I found daring that last big drop of yolk to prove me wrong.

Before I could recall the thought of shoving the waiting remains toward my mouth, the drop fell.

Right on to my shirt nestled against the third button from the top and spreading fast.

"Slob!"

"Taylor tells me that all the time."

I tried a swipe at my shirt to remove or, more likely, smear the yellow glob but found Salem's hand in the way. I thought about brushing her hand off; I wasn't a little kid. But I held it back when Salem gave me the look and began dapping at my chest with a damp napkin.

Undoubtedly, Salem did a better job than me, leaving nothing behind but a wet spot.

I usually left a stain that never seemed to come all the way out, but at that moment, I think the loss of another shirt might have been better than the dapping. It didn't take much of a touch from Salem to get me wondering if I was indeed too old.

Lucky for me, our Ms. Sunshine came back with her working frown back in action. It wasn't exactly an interruption, but it hurried along the cleaning up and gave me something else to think about, both of which were good things.

CHAPTER FIFTEEN

T he familiar frown did not get any friendlier as our waitress returned. She was just in time to watch Salem put the final touches into my cleanup. It was only after Salem began slipping back into her seat that the waitress made a big deal out of placing our bill on the table.

I held my tongue in cheek while our waitress went through the well-rehearsed motions of shuffling the used dishes and napkins into a single stack. She kept it on the edge of the table even as she decided our table needed a wipedown.

She went through the complete wipedown, even though we were still seated.

It didn't take a genius to realize she wanted our table now.

While I had enjoyed her recent softening, there was little doubt we were still not her favorite customers. Yet clearly, a little common courtesy should not have been out of the question.

But we didn't get any.

She should have at least left after the last shadow of a crumb had been whisked away. I sat there with my mouth shut, expecting her to leave, but she stayed tableside, all the while maintaining an impatient two-step back and forth next to our booth as if her pants were full of fire ants.

"Would you like anything else?"

That was a new question for her, or maybe I had forgotten a few things before. After all, that last visit had been several years ago.

Salem shook her head as an answer for both of us.

"Was everything all right?"

"No complaints."

Except you are still hanging around. But I didn't voice that part out loud.

Still, our sourpuss waitress hesitated.

Maybe she was too self-absorbed to realize we were waiting for her departure to finish our talk. We couldn't develop an escape route with her hanging over our heads.

But even if our server left with the dirty dishes, I had to admit we were running out of ideas. It looked more and more like we were going to have to put Salem's paranoia to the test, a move that was definitely not on the top of my to-do list. But what else could we do?

"I am sorry about the eggs."

Where did that come from, and even worse why did she raise her voice to tell us? Her voice wasn't loud enough to reach our buddies in the front, but it got the attention of a couple of nearby tables and wouldn't take much more to reach all the corners of the café.

"Here, let me fix the wrong-style eggs on your check."

I made the effort to shoot my hand out to block her action. But for being such an old crab, our waitress's hand speed was excellent. It probably came from scooping up tips before people could change their minds about leaving one.

I gave up and sat back hard against the wall of the booth. By now I was willing to pay extra just to get the pesky lady to go away and leave us alone. I might have even added a bigger tip if that would have helped.

Thank heaven.

It wouldn't have.

When she plumped the bill down a second time, almost in my lap, I found a grouping of letters in sight rather than numbers. When I got over my surprise, I silently read out the last message I would have expected to find: "When the giggle girls at the next table over get up, do the same and go out through the kitchen."

It took me reading it a second time to realize her second harsher script. It was where she had added, "Your meals are comped by the cook. It will teach him to call in sick."

I pushed the note over toward Salem and mouthed out a silent "Thank you," and she bobbed a "Your welcome" in return.

Now as our waitress walked away, I exchanged a knowing look with Salem. Neither of us had a lot of trust in the woman, but we had little choice but to take her offer.

"I guess you think I am being paranoid?"

I thought about letting Salem stew in her own growing paranoia, but being a male, I stepped forward to offer the damsel a bit of relief.

"Not really. Fears are like wolves, they run in packs." As I uttered the words, my thoughts went out to include the men up front. "Just like hates run together in some nutcases."

CHAPTER SIXTEEN

The three girls sitting across us were older than Taylor but still a bit short of college-dorm age. If I was guessing, I would have figured they were on a last-minute shopping trip before their senior year in high school.

After yet another round of giggles, I had to consider they were just hanging out to gossip about their classmates missing the trip. Either way, when they got tired of their giggling, I could only hope the girls were headed home to change.

Their jeans could have been tighter, but only if they had gotten someone to paint them on. Taylor might have been holding a pair like that in her closet, but only if it was labeled outgrown and ready for the donate box.

Taylor was a real follower of the holes in blue-jean club, but hers were a lot more material than skin. Not so sure that could be said for these girls.

Their tops were a little better. They were loose enough to be comfortable. Yet two of the tops had another uplift to change bumps into mounds, and the third girl with dyed red-streak hair didn't need any help.

All in all, the girls were dressed for attention, which, I'm sure, any teenage boy with the slightest interest in girls would have given them. Hell, a lot of guys my age would have taken that same interest.

"They're too young."

"For who?"

"You and every other guy in this place."

Considering her own past, Salem's voice held a lot of disgust.

"Even the misguided by the door?"

"Especially them!" Salem swirled around the remaining six drops of orange juice in the bottom of her glass before adding with more cat hiss than words, "If I had my way, they would spend the rest of their lives speaking with a much higher voice."

"That sounds a bit racist."

Salem gave me a long look before giving out with an evil-predator snarl, "I would have wished the same and even worse on the Father and his followers. And they were white like you."

White, but not really like me.

But I knew better than to say it out loud.

Whether simple truth or a lot of pent-up guilt, it was hard to tell with Salem. The way she spat out the words like hardened pellets of steel was enough to back me off from asking. After all, it was not that long ago Salem had helped deliver an uncountable number of girls to the Father.

Those young ones had been much younger and a lot more innocent than these girls. Among them all, only Taylor had reached her teen years.

So, if our Ms. Salem had any human DNA in her heart at all, I could see where she carried a lot of guilt.

Although even now, I was not quite sure why Salem had helped us the first time. Taylor claimed it was because of how much she cared about us. Me? At times I wondered if we weren't just a means to escape from the Father's control.

Even this time, Salem had only searched us out in fear of a possible rebirth of the Witch Rose, one Salem claimed might be even more evil than the Father who had fed away the future of a young child every couple of years to the rose.

My eyes came away from Salem to glance down toward the door of the café.

I couldn't imagine anything worse than the Father and his group. But if these men were the extremists Salem suggested, their type had already brought a lot of death and misery into our world. With them in charge of the Witch Rose, it might mean the end of even more futures, young and old.

About then my thinking was dragged back to the present. The gigglers started putting down some money on the table and gathering up their stuff to leave.

CHAPTER SEVENTEEN

I did a quick chug of the remaining six drops in my orange juice glass and slipped to the very edge of the booth. Once there with half my bottom hanging in midair, I held up a hand to keep Salem from sliding into sight.

Leaning out even further, I watched the girls strut toward the door.

Living with Taylor and having a lot of contact with her friends when they were visiting or playing sports gave me some insight into teenagers at their best and worst, because of which, I wasn't overly impressed by these girls with their red-carpet walk.

You could not say the same for most of the other men in the place. At least two of the older guys were on the verge of panting like a pair of overheated dogs, while a third was on the edge of tipping his chair over getting a better view.

Still the strangest of the eaters taking notice was a gray-haired old lady. You would have expected disapproval, but what I saw was a once-over deeper than any man could have managed. And it had nothing to do with disapproval.

The girls were really enjoying the attention.

Or at least the girls were until they reached the area of the exit. Once there, the looks were accompanied by verbal comment, which appeared to be less than polite, and a couple of just missing grabs. Even liking most attention, the girls took notice of the possible danger and toned downed their strut to a more reasonable, if not cower, walk.

It was about then that Ms. Sour Face stepped out to wave us out of our booth and into the kitchen. The last I saw of the exiting girls was them trying to squeeze out of the café heads down.

I was tempted to place my nose where it did not belong. But before I could move to defend their teenage honor, I found a hand grabbing my wrist, followed by a tug and command, "Come on, big boy, we have an exit to make."

Going through the kitchen was a trip with us being invisible.

The staff made such a big deal out of not seeing us it seemed to ruin their whole method of working together. If not, I now realize why the service in some places is so slow.

Popping out right into the lobby, Salem and I found it empty of anyone dangerous. There were a few people in sight going about the in and out of their lobby business. But none of them gave us much notice.

The only other people in sight were a couple of staff members, a middle-aged guy manning the desk and a young kid dressed as a bellboy. Both were more or less helping people.

The desk guy didn't even give us a look-see as we crossed over toward the doors to our branch of the inn. But once there, we did find the bellhop moving over to greet us with a polite "I need a tip" smile as he swung open the door.

Coming through on the way to breakfast, I had pegged the boy as a college kid making summer money. Now on a closer look, the kid looked to be more on the sly side, like a high schooler or, more likely, a dropout.

Either way, opening a door for us was not really a tip-worthy affair until he added my next shocker to my day. "I got the rest of your party settled for you right across the hallway. And if a room connecting to either one of your rooms opens up, I will get you moved."

Right, I am sure bellhops have the power to get us moved.

But at least he seemed to think so.

With the completion of his recital, the kid didn't actually hold out his hand, but it was no longer glued to his side. I should have ignored it, but I didn't.

Bewildered by what the kid was saying, I reached for my wallet and gave him a one with a "Thank you for your help."

Salem hadn't really slowed up her walking with the bellboy's words. She had left me behind and was moving up the steps to our second-floor room before I was finished with the tip.

It took me just short of a run to gain any ground on Salem, and she was well into our hallway before I got any words out.

"Second room?"

"That's what the boy said."

"And you knew about it?"

"Not for sure." Salem went into a nervous step dance, like she needed a restroom in the worse way. "But more than likely."

Their traded looks back in Michigan came back to the forefront.

"Did Taylor call you?"

"No, but I heard about the second room this morning and doubted it was for me." Salem had decided long before our arrival that, considering our relationship status, separate beds would be safe enough for us. "And you cannot blame her. Taylor really wanted to help."

And I really wanted my granddaughter tucked away back in Michigan. I could still remember my last trip out here, and having Taylor sharing the danger was not a part of my deal to help Salem with the Witch Rose.

Maybe it was time to call it all off and head back to Michigan, dragging Ms. Taylor along by her hair if I had to.

CHAPTER EIGHTEEN

Salem read my expression like she would have an extra-large sign hanging over the freeway and tightened her grip on my sleeve.

"Don't kill her."

Not that I would have, but...

"Why not?"

"Because you love her."

I reached down with my right hand to gently pluck my sleeve free from Salem. "Do you really think I could ever hurt Taylor?"

"Physically, no."

Salem leaned back into the wall as if she needed something solid for extra support, almost as if it was a heavy load for her to care about us as people.

"Emotionally, you have the perfect granddaughter-grandfather relationship. That you could kill."

I waffled between anger and what Salem was saying.

"Taylor should have stayed home." Both of my hands went out in front to shake out an added, "She doesn't even have a driver's license."

"Taylor didn't drive here by herself!" Salem's hand reached out like a claw about to scratch my blindness away. "And after what happened here before, you know she wouldn't."

Reminding me of before was not the best way to calm me down. It carried me right past the first part of Salem's comments into "She almost died back then."

"We saved her then, and if needed, we will now as well." Salem's expression softened a bit, almost into a smile. "I know this because I am not explaining to Sandy how we let her daughter get killed."

"I would be more afraid of John. He is a lot bigger."

I turned away from Salem to grab the doorknob of the room across ours and froze.

John was a lot bigger and younger than me, but his ire didn't scare me at all. It was the thought of Junior's spite, being disappointed in his father, which slowed me down.

"All right, I promise no killing or violent touching." I tried for a grin, but it fell as flat as my singing voice. "Do you mind if I yell a lot?"

"If you keep it semiquiet. After all, I don't want to get thrown out of here." A smile would have helped the mood, but Salem was cat serious as she reached past me to turn the knob. "I have had my fill of sleeping in the back of trucks or out of doors."

I thought with that as we were going in, but Salem hesitated one last moment.

And for a moment?

The Salem from long ago came back.

Besides, I need all the help I can get.

CHAPTER NINETEEN

Salem's twisting the knob took forever, and the releasing click of the door thundered through the hallway like a steam engine going through a tunnel. It took all my willpower to hold back from reaching out to pull the door back in place without going in.

Maybe the whole thing was a misunderstanding.

Maybe the bellhop had gotten his information confused.

And maybe the voice floating out from the room was not the familiar "Hi, Dad."

At least it was not the voice I had been expecting.

I mean my daughter should have known better than to have come. Back home, Jess and Jody had agreed with my decision to keep Taylor safe in Michigan. Ordering my daughters themselves to stay at home had never crossed my mind. After all, didn't they have jobs and livings of their own to take care?

Not that ordering them would have done any good.

Junior and I believed in totems.

And if Junior had been the wolf of the family, Jody and Jess were the lionesses—or cougars, depending on their moods and needs. They both carried the leadership gene of a lioness leading a pride of lions across the African plains. No one under their care would ever need for substance or shelter.

Surprisingly enough, my girls were just as strong living on their own like the American cougar. While they enjoyed being with people, it was not an everyday requirement.

I had always known about these qualities in the abstract. But it was Junior who had taken them a step further, attaching them to their proper guardian totem.

But none of that mattered.

I was just overjoyed to find my daughter in the room and not my granddaughter. For a moment, my worst fears were put away. At least Jess was a full-grown adult and had been taking care of herself and others for years.

Better yet, Jess had been doing a fabulous job it.

"Hi, kid." I sank into Jess's hug out of fatherly habit and drank in the well-known smell of her lavender shampoo. "You shouldn't have come."

"Remembering your stories about this place, I thought my dad might need some help and somebody had to drive." The hug back felt even better than habit. "Jody would have been here as well but couldn't take off at a moment's notice as easy as me."

Jess shouldn't have said all that.

Something about somebody sounded too much like a plural road trip instead of the singular "I came along to help you all by myself" thing, especially if there was no chance of her twin coming along.

I felt my recent breakfast going back into a Gordian knot, and I didn't have one of Alexander the Great's swords handy.

"And of course, your sister also had to stay home to watch over Taylor."

"Well..." My daughter's cheeks rolled up to squint her eyes, a move I had seen at least a million times in the past few decades, usually leading up to something I didn't want to know.

But this time, Jess didn't get a chance to add anything on.

Because at that very moment of buildup, I saw a pair of blue shorts matched up with a T-shirt from University of Michigan, a tee that was damp around the neckline from where an expansive mop of damp blond hair had brushed across as it was wrapped in a towel for drying, all of which popped out of the bathroom with the last grin I wanted to see here in Pennsylvania.

CHAPTER TWENTY

Losing my cool did a lot of good.

Two of the three girls rode out my sputtering with a pair of "heard it all before" grins, knowing full well they had the upper hand with the fact-accomplished argument, which, when mentioned, did nothing but reheat my sputtering into a second extended round.

But in the end, I was outnumbered two and a half to one.

I held Salem down to a half credit against, since instead of taking sides, she had retired to the windowsill. She appeared to ignore our confrontation by soaking up the sunshine, but the perkiness of Salem's ears said "I am listening." To me, it felt like Salem was reinforcing their position by adding nothing to mine.

I finally left the room with the ice bucket as an excuse. Outside the room, I directed the steaming fume at myself and the world—mostly myself, because I must have done a terrible job of raising my kids.

You would think by now they would have learned to listen to me. After all, I was their elder.

Growing up, the girls, they listened.

At least a lot better than Junior, but I had to admit they had their moments.

Come to think of it, since there were two of them, there were a lot of moments.

And now?

I had to admit that Jody and Jess were now adults.

They were working girls in charge of other people at their respective jobs and more used to giving out orders than taking. I should probably have made myself clearer about them following my commands to the letter, but even then, I am not sure it would have mattered.

Taylor, on the other hand, was another matter.

She was a minor under my care.

She was a teenager living in my home.

And we had shared a once-in-a-lifetime nightmare on a nearby mountainside. If watching her raging grandpa swinging a war ax around like a berserk maniac hadn't permanently scared Taylor with a fear of me, nothing would.

In hindsight, after putting that all together, I should never have expected her to listen to my order to stay at home.

But I had.

I filled up the ice bucket and then leaned into the ice machine for support.

How mad should I be?

Taylor was basically a good kid who carried exceptionally good grades and so far had skipped over the "I hate you" stage with me, maybe not as perfectly with Sandy and John. From what they had relayed to me, they had not been as lucky. There had been more than one instance of teen angst, usually coming in connection with the word "no."

And even if Taylor was a total brat, shouldn't I cut her some slack with this situation?

Taylor had already gone through more shit at six in a single night than most people would ever see in a hundred-year lifetime.

Thinking it over?

It was better to go along with fact accomplish than to add another thing to her outhouse accumulation.

The same could not be said for the people I found waiting outside my room upon my return from the ice machine.

CHAPTER TWENTY-ONE

There were four of them.

The foursome was made up of two men and a woman who appeared to be carrying a toddler in a brightly colored backpack-style carrier. The SpongeBob carrier didn't look all that comfortable for either one involved, but what did I know? It had been quite a while since I had carried around a child so young.

And when I did, I used to carry them piggyback up on my shoulders when they were younger than this one.

So who was I to judge?

The two guys looked rather bland with bodies that had never enjoyed the get-in-shape exhaustion of a high school sports team. While the lady wasn't much better, she had a plain face locked in a permanent scowl with, at best, an average body form. You might have gotten the body form upgraded with a gym-style toning.

The toddler looked to be the brightest of the four, and as babies went, he or she was rather dull-looking with a round expressionless face.

Clothes-wise, they were all sporting inexpensive outfits that screamed lack of imagination. I had seen more bright colors in a winter snowstorm.

Put it all together, they looked more stupid than dangerous.

Still, I smelled trouble all the same.

After all, they were knocking on my door, and they were definitely not members of the staff.

"Can I help you?"

Everybody but the toddler took a quick measure of me, and without exception, they were all equally unimpressed. I am not sure if it was because of my age or the tiny, little ice bucket in my right hand.

The best response they could spare was a dismissing smile from the woman. Then she went quickly back to a knuckle rap on my door.

"Are you sure I can't help?"

The flabbier of the two still maintained "ignore the pest and he will go away." But his friend had a different take on my intrusion.

He gave me a "none of your business" look and began to vocalize an answer as well. But before it came out, the woman's hand came away from the knocking to latch on to his forearm with an unspoken command.

"No thank you"—the lady's voice was almost pleasant—"we are just here to pick up a visitor."

"Maybe I can help you." I nodded my head in a general down-the-hall nod. "I have been staying just over there and have seen most of the men coming and going. Maybe I can tell you if he is in."

"Not likely." Her tone was cooling off with each new utterance. "Our friend is a woman."

When I made no move to walk away, the lady gave out a deep-rooted sigh. After a complete round of my heartbeat, she continued, fighting like mad to hold on to the last of her faked pleasantness.

"She has silver hair and green eyes."

"Oh, and before you go any further, I need to tell you one more thing." I reached out to nudge the lady's hand away from the knocking. "This is my room, and I am the only one staying here."

"You lie!"

Again, the hothead of the group made an effort to take command of the situation, but for the second time, the woman's grasp reached out for his forearm. Only this time, she added a look, gentle but firm.

"You don't understand"—she reached with her free hand to gesture to me—"we need to talk to her. My friends and I are doing God's work."

I tilted my head to one side in mock interest. "By any chance does your God's work include the protesting of military funerals?"

CHAPTER TWENTY-TWO

The woman's arm thumped to her side.

Then my face became the all-encompassing center of her gaze. What was left of the smile faded away like the turnoff of a flashlight. The eyes about that smile showed how I was moving right up the ladder from bothersome local to another misinformed member of the public.

Given my present attitude and mood with Taylor's sudden presence, I could see myself working the title all the way up to complete pain in the ass with the next minute or so.

"That military is supporting a homosexual-loving government." I could actually see the fanatic's chest pump up with each word. "Which everyone knows is a sin against humanity."

"I don't!"

She started to roll out a second memorized sermon, but I held her off with a single upraised finger.

"To my way of thinking, those boys died protecting you and me from our enemies, both foreign and domestic."

I made sure to put an extra hard beat on the word *domestic*, and they all noticed, including the toddler. The leader's eyes were the biggest reaction, snapping wide to meet mine.

As supposedly an intelligent adult, I should have let it drop and retreated into my room beyond their reach. After all, there is nothing I could say to sway them from their chosen path.

So of course, I poured on the fuel.

"My son was one of those who served."

"Was?"

While the woman in charge picked up on my word use, the moron leaning forward from off to my side did not.

"Good, I'll pray extra hard for his death."

Maybe the arrogant moron didn't know any better, but I had had enough of today's crap.

Without thinking about it, I made sure this particular ass would be doing his praying without teeth, several pieces of which went popping across the carpet like dice thrown at the casino, right after my recently filled ice bucket made contact with the junction between his ear and cheek.

It could not have been a more perfect strike since it was aided by his need to lean forward with his taunt. And to make it worse, under my current mood, I was in deep thought over adding a face stomp as his head bounced sideways off the floor.

But first I had to make sure his companions were not about to get involved during my dropkick practicing. The last thing I needed was to be taken out by an attack from the rear.

The woman might have been the leader of this group. But for once, it seemed she remembered the child on her back and retreated out of ice bucket range.

Her remaining escort wasn't going to win an award for the quickest backup in the world. He stood there stunned into a statue mode, which pretty much left him defenseless. I could have finished him off with the remaining portion of the ice bucket, but I didn't get a chance.

Before I could shift my grip on the ice bucket handle, a voice came out of the air from behind my side of the conflict.

"I saw your friend slip on the ice, and I would hate to see one of you have the same problem."

Slow-witted or not, the remaining male member of the group needed only a half look at the owner of the voice to decide his course of action.

Not that I blamed the guy.

I had already rattled him with my burst of sudden violence, and now he had a canyon-deep voice thrown in as well, one belonging to a man casting a huge shadow, which had me backpedaling a step myself, even as I found myself hoping he was on my side.

After taking a second measure of the voice, Mr. Flabby Mute added another notch of speed to his withdrawal. He was almost to the corner before I got out the obvious question.

"Aren't you forgetting your friend?"

I guess not.

He halted the retreat but made no move to advance back in our direction.

It was left to the female of the group to aid her broken-jawed protestor. Yet hampered by the baby pack, there was little she could do to get the jaw-holding crier on his feet. Their retreat became a half-aided crawl with a lot of moaning and very little speed.

The couple might have still been there if not for Mr. Gutless finally figuring out there was enough room for a quick grab of his friend without major danger.

So with his help, the woman was able to get the injured jerk to his feet for a drunk man's stumbling retreat down the hallway.

They were just about to turn into the hallway leading back toward the exit when the woman hesitated. She held the others back, gave for a final look in my direction.

And even at the distance of her retreat, I could read the expression.

Plain as day, it said in her mind: "This was not the way things were supposed to happen in my world."

CHAPTER TWENTY-THREE

About then, two men carrying briefcases came around the same corner. Since they were looking back as they rounded the corner, there was little chance of them missing the parade going down the hall.

Claiming I knew nothing about the circus they had just passed didn't seem plausible. I would have had to be hooked up to a seeing eye dog to miss their passing.

And explaining their present condition away would have been hard enough under normal circumstances. But to make the situation way beyond normal, I was dangling a badly dented ice bucket from one hand, with, of course, an assortment of melting ice and broken teeth scattered around the carpet in from of my door.

The briefcases screamed businessmen coming back from an early morning meeting or working breakfast. Since there were no ties in sight, I was guessing the latter.

As the two men shifted their stares from their recent back path to me, I knew I was in trouble. I had been lucky enough to share an empty hall with the religious nutcases during my recent ice bucket-swinging incident.

But I should have known my luck would not last.

Still maybe in one way, it had.

The two interlopers checking us out from their position at the head of the hall hesitated between challenge and flight. It was about then my guardian's voice again came to my rescue.

"The injured one tried to grab our wallets and run off with them"—the voice added an arm sweep at the floor to go with his finish—"but the bucket got turned over with his grab and he slipped on the ice."

Since I was holding an ice bucket with the side caved in and had a collection of broken bits of teeth scattered around the carpet at my feet, my benefactor's story leaked more water than my ice bucket.

From the looks on their faces, I didn't see them believing it either. But at the same time, there was also the absence of doubt I expected. Mostly, there was just a big measuring of us, with most of the gauging being centered on my partner in crime.

"Should we?"

The voice waved the lead businessman's question away before it really got started.

"I'll take care of informing the desk personnel. I do a little part-time security for the inn."

I still didn't see a lot of belief in their faces.

But in the end, the pair did a lot of nodding as they moved on toward their rooms. As they passed us, I doubt if there was more than an inch between their shoulders and the far wall.

Once they had worked their way past my new friend and me, their speed picked up measurably. And as they reached their room just short of the end of hall, it took three fumbles and a drop before they got the door unlocked. Then and only then did they give the voice standing next to me a final glance and heavy headshake before disappearing into their room, finally giving me a chance for a real survey of the voice.

Once started, I could see why they had made a point of nodding so many times. I would have done the same and quite likely added on a head to the ground bow as well.

The helping voice must have been at least six feet, six inches tall with a weight of around the three-hundred-pound mark, none of which looked to be fat.

Most of his face was covered by a thick mat of raven hair that would have made an ancient Viking proud. It was accompanied by more glistening of the same drawn back into a matching ponytail that draped itself halfway down his back.

The facial features between the darken strands were strong and reeked of power, all of which were overseen by a pair of blue eyes blessed with the ice-cold clearness of the north.

Once done checking him out, I had to ask, "Are you a Norse god or what?"

CHAPTER TWENTY-FOUR

"**A**n 'or what.'"

We shared a laugh at his answer, and I stuck out my hand to the giant.

"Thanks for your help."

"No problem, but not sure you're the one who needed it." Without releasing our handshake, the dark giant reached out with his other hand to finger the flatten ice bucket. He seemed to be gauging the bucket's thickness with a warrior appreciation. "If this thing was any thicker, my help would have had to include hiding a body."

"He might have hit a sore spot."

I held off his answer as I did a bucket check of my own. The metal was pretty much folded in on itself, like the flattened Coke cans you found in the streets.

It had me wondering about my reaction—not whether the bucket swing was right or wrong, but on how easy I had slipped back into the violence of our mountainside adventure. It felt almost like I enjoyed hitting the fanatic.

Without time for more introspection, I gave the immense man another once-over.

After all, grateful or not, I had to wonder about his help. Most people would have sided with a kidding, holding woman and her injured accomplice. Either that, or avoided the situation completely.

Had he overheard the conversation from the beginning?

I didn't think so, but it would explain his choice of sides.

The church my visitors represented was not the most popular one in this country, especially If you were in the military or had a family member serving.

For all I knew, my savior might have a family member of his own in Arlington or one of its cousin graveyards scattered around the country. If so, his actions made complete sense.

In any case, I could not let Salem's paranoia influence my every action. There was no way everybody in the town was against us.

Still, it didn't hurt to ask.

"If you don't mind me asking, why did you take my side?"

"Had to." The voice pointed toward Junior's dog tags hanging loose on my chest as he pulled an even heavier silver chain up out of his own shirt. "We have to take care of our own."

"Your military?"

"Hardly." The Norseman bellowed out a giant-sized laugh and hauled the chain free of his neckline and into the open. It sported a pentagram twice the size of mine. "I am a believer from the old country."

Okay.

So I was wrong, and Salem was right, again.

Everybody in this town was against us.

And now the question became "Should I lie to the big fellow about my situation? Or should I take a chance on him accepting who I was without trying to remove my head as he made a move to grab Salem?"

I took another look at his hands.

Yep, those hands looked big enough to twist off the head of a steer, and my head was a lot smaller than that. Still I couldn't just stand here. I had to say something.

"The chain is mine, but the symbols and tags belonged to my son."

"So you yourself are a Christian."

His smile didn't fade at all, but it somehow seemed to hold less glow. And the chain with the symbol of his beliefs made a quick disappearance back behind the beard and into his shirt.

"Not like those"—I bobbed my head toward the far end of the hall—"still, I guess I am as close to being Christian as anything else. But I have always figured there were a number of things from the Native Americans we could learn from."

"That there is." The big guy accompanied his short comment with a chest pat down to make sure the chain had dropped back into place. And then he let out a supersized sigh and relaxed the smile off his face.

It was almost a return to normal before he asked, "Your son?"

CHAPTER TWENTY-FIVE

"**B**uried in Arlington." I tightened my grip around Junior's dog tags until I could almost read the raised letters of his name and blood type. "He chose to follow your ways shortly before leaving for Iraq."

"Did you approve?"

"Not really, but it was Junior's life and I respected his judgment."

The man straightened up tall and gave the expression on my face a long study as he chewed over the words of my answer. And then his huge paw came forward to swallow mine in another handshake, this one a bit firmer and longer with words.

"Then I chose the right side."

Before I got anything else out, the big guy was disappearing around the corner and out of sight. It was only then I realized there had never been an exchange of names.

Of course, it didn't really matter; I would have bet my last half dollar on his identity even without his name. But I was also sure Salem would have that information stolen away. It would only take a brief rendition of my recent confrontation to bring it out.

But before going back into the girl's room, I studied the floor, wondering to myself if I should try to clean up the mess or leave the ice to melt and soak into the carpet on its own.

Only the extra key card lying to one side brought me up short with another question.

The room number on the card matched my door, but a quick pocket check proved it wasn't mine.

71

I tried hoping it had been dropped by Salem, but knowing my cat lady's calculated behavior, I didn't see that happening.

I was beginning to think I needed to have a long talk with a certain bellboy. Maybe he could tell me what the accepted rate was for giving out room cards to nonguests.

"I'm pretty sure the woman of the group dropped it when you redesigned her companion's jaw."

Bringing my sight line up from the floor, I found a pair of heads. They were sticking out from the opposing door one above the other.

"Were you, by any chance, watching through the peephole?"

"We took turns after Salem heard them knocking at your door." Taylor let the door edge open enough for her to check out the hall way in either direction. "I tried to get you a text message warning, but you came back too soon."

I didn't know whether to verbally slap Salem for not coming to my aid or bless Taylor for having the common sense to stay safely in their room instead of rushing out headfirst into the confrontation.

Probably I would do both before the end of the day.

But more importantly, it was over for the moment and everyone was in one piece.

I thanked God for that as Jess joined the other two in the doorway.

Jess had mentioned needing a shower as I was leaving for the ice. Not sure how far she had gotten with the idea. But since Jess's blouse was soaking wet, she had at least gotten started on her hair.

I tried to gather them all into a wide hug for an easing back into the room. But before I got them gathered, Taylor gave out the first of my coming questions.

"Were those your bastards from out west?"

Salem gave her an instantaneous nod as I added on the obvious.

"And the big guy is your pagan?"

This time, we didn't get a quick nod or even a slow one.

Instead we got Salem moving out into the hall to pick up a large piece of broken tooth from the carpet. She turned it over in a two-fingered examination as if finding a missing filling or a secret mark to identity the owner was the most important thing in her world.

Only Salem's eyes were not really seeing the broken tooth.

They were at least a million miles away, reviewing something out of sight or buried in Salem's past.

I was not sure which.

CHAPTER TWENTY-SIX

Of course, being confused about Salem's thoughts was nothing new to our relationship.

To begin with, Salem was a woman. To date, my record of understanding the fairer sex was less than perfect or even worth a passing grade, for that matter.

When you added on Salem's perchance for leaning toward the feline side of her behavior, it moved the marker from failing grade to shit out of luck.

Usually, about now was when I came up with a stupid question to seal my fate as a male pig, but not this time. I held off in what looked like the mature-thing-to-do manner. But to tell the truth, I could not think of a single thing to say.

To maintain my stance of wisdom, I backed off from the girl's side of the hall to take a position of ease, the one where I leaned back into the locked door of my room and took up a casual interest in Salem's contemplation.

On the other side of the hallway, Taylor was giving Jess a rapid-fire recap of what had happened.

It seemed starting in on her shower with a shampooing had forced Jess to delay long enough to get out and half dry off, or a delay just long enough for Jess to miss my momentary lack of control.

It was only when Taylor finished her fill-in that I realized how much of the confrontation I had missed. Among them the fact that I had intimidated the Norse god so badly he had been forced to slink away in fear.

About then, Salem came back into our universe.

"Your savior was the right size and shape but the wrong age." Salem made a big deal of flipping the fragment toward the end of the hall. "The pagan I dodged had a gray braid and beard even longer than your new friend's."

"Could the Witch Rose be changing him?"

I let my mind backtrack to the mountainside.

The father and his followers had stayed young for decades or, in the case of the Father himself, centuries. All through the power of the Witch Rose and paid for with the potential of little ones way too young to be used as sacrifices.

About then it dawned on me.

That is where Salem's mind had just gone.

Now I could see where Salem's face held on to a slight doubt, even as the words came out as a sure thing.

"Not this time"—Salem's gaze turned on to my face with a complete lack of shadow—"the Witch Rose is years away from being that strong."

"If they force-fed it potentially?"

"Still months at least."

"A follower?"

Salem's eyes came off me to follow the question back to Taylor. They shared an eye contact longer than ours had been, but in the end, the answer was no more fulfilling.

"I don't think so."

After that, Salem's eyes might have come back to mine, but again, they were a million miles or years away. I could only imagine where, but at least this time, the trip was of a shorter duration.

"Yeah"—I got the words out even as Salem began reaching for them—"the guy didn't give off the vibe of a follower."

"Not even the sense of a second-in-command."

For a long moment, our minds shared a common connection where words were not really needed.

An innocent bystander?

The leader of a fourth group?

Or something beyond our imagination?

"There must be a connection"—Taylor cut through our musing and brought us back to the here and now—"someone that big does not just pop out of the ground."

Or did he?

Right now I was not really sure of anything.

CHAPTER
TWENTY-SEVEN

It was time for some information gathering—Information I could get from a computer or sitting here in the inn.

I thought of going it alone, but Jess nixed that with a heavy-handed volunteering.

To be truthful, all three girls put forth a strong willingness to go, but I certainly wasn't ready for a rehash of Taylor's presence at the inn. Salem might have been a better choice, but without an extra-large baseball cap big enough to contain her hair completely, it didn't seem a good idea.

The plan was to drive around and check out sites I remembered from my last visit, the closest of which was Sandy and Taylor's old home.

It hadn't been an impressive structure during their stay in the place.

Now it was even worse.

What had once been a fairly well-kept front yard was now mostly brown dust. The turf that had managed to survive was more an assortment of dandelions and other unwanted weeds than any form of grass, all of which was in bad need of mowing.

Before our night on the mountain, there had been a small flowering trim of Witch Rose vines. They had edged around the front of the house claiming it as their own.

Now, not only were the vines long gone, but they had been replaced by a collection of discarded bottles and cans. With enough littered paper mixed in, the base of the house was turned into a real rat's delight.

The building itself would have looked better paintless with just bare wood. Most people would still have labeled it as a white house, but with most of the paint curled up or peeled off, I think *shack* would have been a more fitting title.

The world would have pegged it an abandoned dump. But it took only one glance from the corner to tell me it was suffering an even worse fate.

Three of the men stationed around on the porch were from the group we had seen at the café this morning. The other two I was seeing for the first time.

All five had adopted what they thought of as an American look, choosing outfits consisting of the summer slacks with causal button-down shirts.

They didn't pull it off.

Their garb was the same as mine in some ways but a lot different in others. I am not sure how to explain it in words most people would understand, but any person who had lived or traveled through the Middle East would have understood.

Three of the misfits were huddled around a chopped-down table, playing what might have been dominoes. I couldn't make out the pieces, but the players were doing a lot of bouncing up and down with a maximum of slamming the table with their hands. Even the fourth member of the group watching from the railing was unable to remain in one position.

Only the fifth and final member of the porch patrol seemed to be ignoring the game. Instead of staying involved with the other, he was standing by himself in front of the porch, smoking a cigarette and giving us the evil eye.

I couldn't blame him for his reaction to our drive-by.

From what Salem had told me during our drive back here, we might be the only people driving past. Apparently, the rest of the community had begun avoiding the place shortly after the new owners had taken possession.

We were more than halfway past the house when I realized the man's evil eye was directed not at us but only Jess. When he realized Jess had noticed his gaze, he gave off a sexual suggestion.

To her credit, my girl, Jess, held her own.

She did so by using an age-old single-digit expression to convey her negative opinion to the man.

CHAPTER TWENTY-EIGHT

"Not the toughest-looking group I've ever seen."

"You're right." I spared a final glance into my rearview mirror and again had doubts about my daughter's choice of covered street-wise news when needed. "But being true believers probably gives them an extra altitude of danger all the same."

"Right, but remember, Dad, so are we." Next to me, Jess made a big deal of not looking back. "After all, we have a cat on our side."

"Cat or lion?"

Jess gave off a crooked smile at the mention of her totem. Of my twins, she was the one who clung to the little remembrances of her brother. With her sister, Jody, preferring to avoid the subject, saying such things brought back a stab of hurt each time they were brought up.

Jody's one exception came when questioned by Taylor.

Jody and Jess had done their best to bring the memory of Junior alive for Taylor, no matter how bad it hurt, and according to Jess, some of the questions brought up tear-jerking replies.

"Both!" The lag in answering brought a jerk up straight from me, almost hard enough to drag my one tire into the curb. "And we also have Ms. Taylor added in for good measure."

Remembering that fact didn't help the conversation. "What about me?"

"Well, you are old and male." I knew inside that Jess didn't really mean it, with her grin beyond evil to downright mean. "But we might need someone to pick up any spilled ice."

"I knew I should have drowned you at birth and kept your sister."

"Sure thing, like my sister would be treating you any better."

"Probably not."

I made a show of my own, hesitating for a long moment before answering, "I should have made it a group drowning and saved myself a ton of money for my own enjoyment."

"Really!"

"Naw, I had too much fun watching you two grow up." I took my eyes off the road for a two-beat eye hold. "But Jody is still my favorite."

Jess's swing might have come at me as an off-sided backhand, but it still thudded in with a solid rib plunk. The blow might have even interfered with my driving if I had not been expecting it.

To tell the truth, I would have been more upset if Jess had reacted any other way.

Our banter might have seemed natural enough to most people, but Jess's voice had carried more than a hint of tightness. Hopefully, the banter and punch had loosened it up somewhat.

"Let's go check out the Father's place of worship."

"Sure, kid." I made the left turn en route to the residence of the Father's evil. "At least that building cannot be any worse than the house."

So of course, I was wrong.

The grass was mowed golf green prefect, and the few windows in sight were so clean I could imagine birds flying into them by mistake. It was the people scattered around the area who were the problem.

The two closest were adult females dressed Midwest American enough. Perhaps a bit conservative for their age.

Hell, when I took a second look, I saw they were dressed too conservatively for any age, and I outranked them in the age department by several decades. In contrast, my daughter would have picked blue jeans for their present chore.

At the moment, the ladies looked to be babysitting three little boys playing in the grass, none of whom could have been more than four, yet they were already condemned to a life of hate.

It only took a slow drive down the length of Father's old place to confirm that belief.

There were two more adults at the far end, one of each sex, perched at the entrance end of the building. Like their companions down toward the corner, they were also dressed in colorless outfits.

Only theirs were more like work clothes from the last century and they had paintbrushes in their hands. I doubt they were working on anything new, as it seemed to be more of a touch-up job.

Personally, I think they should have skipped the touch-up and gone straight to the bonfire.

"Homosexuality is a sin against God."

"Our government is damned for their support of gays."

"This soldier died for queers."

"Praying for another soldier to die."

The silence next to me was even more biting than the sentiment of the signs. When Jess finally broke it, the words came out cracked and broken.

"That doesn't say much for Christianity."

My look told me Jess was doing her best to dig her nails through my cupholders. While Jess wasn't the best of churchgoers, she did lean toward a tolerance toward all.

"All religions have their nutcases."

"Why?"

"Because they are good at it."

I had more wisdom to add, but I never added it. I found the nearest spot out of sight of the haters and parked the Ranger.

"Daddy, Junior was my brother!"

A fight, a breakup, or even the worst of divorces—you can handle by marching forward toward the chance of another love. But with a death, there was no such hope, just a deep loss. Maybe worse when the one taken was too young, violently and out of the natural course of life.

All I could do was hold Jess while she shook out her anger with heavy sobs.

CHAPTER TWENTY-NINE

The graveyard showed me nothing.

The graves were still in place; my memory was a bit on the lacking side.

I couldn't be sure if it was the second grave in the third row or the third plot in the second row that I was looking for.

Or perhaps neither.

I remembered an angel draped heavily by the Witch Rose vines, but which one? From here I could see three of them, all within the possible range of my last visit.

"Would walking around inside help?"

I shook my head and took a last look around the grounds.

There might have been some unseen vines near the bases of the gravestones, but since the grass was badly in need of cutting, there was no way to be 100 percent sure.

I could come back at night when the vines would be blossoming, but something told me I would not find anything more after dark.

Checking out two of the houses I had remembered as having an infestation of well showed me the same. So if nothing else? When you added it all up, there was the plantless condition of the house with the too-clean walls of the onetime center of Father's power, and now this. I was at least sure in my own mind that the Witch Rose itself had not gotten strong enough to reach out into the city as of today.

Jess was the one to come up with the next question on the agenda.

"Now where?"

I gave my daughter a long look before shifting my Ranger into gear. It took Jess a half block to speak out, but only speaking when she was sure there was no better answer.

"You going up there again?"

"Yep."

"Daddy..." The strain of Jess's early outburst was still present in her voice. Not so much as a sound, but in a tenor only a father or sibling might catch. "You're too old."

"I was too old the last time."

"And you've added another eight years on that."

"Good thing the Witch Rose did not wait much longer, or I would be downright ancient."

"I have heard your taste in music." With each new comment, I heard the bit of stress easing away. "You are already ancient!"

"Thanks, kid." I tried sticking my tongue out in Jess's direction but was not sure if it was seeable. "Glad to know you think I have finally grown beyond the immature age."

"You haven't." I heard the last bit of stress easing away. "But that's okay. We love you anyway."

I thought about it for a moment and then went with my twin's favorite comment.

"Awesome!"

The poke in my arm told me things were headed back to normal. With this in mind, I figured this was a good time to break away for some calorie intake.

A cell phone call to our room informed the others of our intent, and we all agreed to meet at Taylor's childhood haunt. Whether we finally ate there or not depended on if Taylor's old friend and owner was working the place.

"She wasn't."

CHAPTER THIRTY

"Nobody was."

Well, not exactly nobody.

Jess and I got to the eatery, while Salem was in the process of dismissing an ancient taxi from the curbside. Just a minute or two too late to prevent the look seizing Taylor's face.

Even before leaping out of the Ranger, I saw the combination of horror, shock, loss, and sadness wash over Taylor's innocence. The only thing not there were the emotions from the happiness family.

Salem's own expression was locked into a catlike stoicism, but just maybe there was still a trace of disgust or loss around the edge.

Not sure which.

Mine, I don't want to know.

The diner was still there, but not in its previous state.

In my memory, Mel's Place had been a step beyond a well-maintained eatery. It wasn't hard to tell the front of the building got a scrape and repaint job every summer. And as for the windows, they had been kept so clean you could have turned the glass sideways and eaten off it. Mel was so fussy she would not allow a fly speck of dirt to rest on them for more than a half second.

According to Sandy, Taylor's mother, Mel, the owner of the eatery, had once chased down a couple of teenage vandals. Once caught, they decided to go back and clean off their handiwork to the owner's specifications.

Now!

Pieces of plywood covered over what once had been the wall-length window showing the inner delights of the diner to any passerby who cared to look. There was also another single plank doing the same for the door. All the boards were framed in by the blackened streaks of destruction.

"Gas explosion."

"Recently?" Or was it something Salem had forgotten to mention?

"Just last week." The speaker stepped forward to point at the door. "Luckily, it went off before they had a chance to open for breakfast or the loss of life would have been worse than Mel and the two girls who always helped her open up."

Our informer was retired from the local police force and even older than me. He was sure to point out how he didn't often talk to a stranger, and I almost told him I usually didn't listen to them neither.

But we both would have been lying.

Either way, this guy claimed to be a regular who ate his lunch here every day. While on the other hand, I had not been to Mel's since my visit years ago, which made him the expert on local happening.

According to the police reports, the diner had suffered a gas leak leading to an explosion. As such, there was no need for any further investigation.

Our new friend didn't agree.

He blamed it on the Arabs and their terrorist ways. His explanation came out a lot stronger and long-winded, but it boiled down to the same message.

I might have written his version off to small-town racism but for few facts. One of the facets of his story was that both the Arabs and the group from the church had been hanging around asking questions about Salem's whereabouts.

The retired officer claimed Mel had shrugged off the questions with her standard reply of "eat or leave." Finally, in a moment of self-righteousness, Mel had banned both groups for life.

Everybody, including the local police, accepted Mel's decision as final. But according to our friend, both groups had hung around across the street to keep the diner under surveillance during working hours.

It seemed like each group was afraid the other would get a foot up on them in their search for Salem.

It stayed a mutual standoff until a tall man with a dark ponytail and beard had showed up. He had stayed for a full day exchanging a never-ending chatter with Mel.

For once, the members of both groups had worked together in an effort to keep the pair of them in sight from across the street. According to the old man, they had given the ponytailed man enough nasty glares to peel the makeup off Mary Poppins.

Two mornings later, Mel's place blew up.

CHAPTER THIRTY-ONE

Thirty minutes after our graphic fill-in at the diner, Jess and I were pulling into the inn's parking lot, with Jess, and probably me to a lesser degree, having gained a brand-new grasp of the situation.

While our staying in the realm of public sight had seemed less than ideal to begin with, now it began to feel downright stupid.

"Do you think it was a planned explosion?"

"Has to be," Taylor and Salem answered in unison from the open window positions they had claimed as we entered the lot. "Mel would have smelled a gas leak."

"But the police report…" Jess left the rest unsaid as she took in the looks on ours faces. After all, she was a believer in the police and had never seen the Father's onetime influence here.

"I don't think we can count on the local police." Jess gave me a questioning look from under the McDonald's bags on her lap in the passenger side of the Ranger. "Looking the other way is not an easy habit to break."

"The Father was that powerful?"

"That creepy!"

Surprisingly, it was Salem who shook her head in my direction. "More than just creepy, Father was that evil."

Jess's face lost more than a little color, and I watched a shiver run like a wave down the entire length of her body, including her hair and toes.

"You want to go home?"

"Yes, it's scary here." Jess picked the lunch bags up one at a time to hand out the window to Taylor. "But only after we have finished helping Salem."

Salem pulled her elbows off my opened window to allow its return to an upright and closed position. Then as I joined my girls gathering in front of the Ranger, Jess brought up the second part of the discussion.

"Still, I can see where the police would have a hard time believing a church group would blow up a diner."

"You think they did it?"

Personally, I was going with the Arab connection. After all, they did have a long international history of terrorism.

"They were the ones confronting you in the hall." Jess began a climb toward our rooms on the outside stairs. "To me, they seem a lot more dangerous than the guys we saw standing on the porch of Sandy's former home."

"And you think about it"—Taylor grabbed a french fry out of the bag she was carrying and chunked it into her mouth as she finished—"Mel treated me like a little princess, but even then, she had little patience for idiots."

True.

I had seen her get under the Father's skin when he was doing his best to come off as friendly and nice. And I knew he probably leaned toward that type of solution.

So even if I didn't like the timing aspect, I couldn't dismiss the stray-nut theory, especially in a town that had lived under the evil influence of the Witch Rose.

And if you thought about it, our Norse god had been part of the story. Maybe he had gotten everything he needed out of Mel and didn't want to take a chance on sharing.

Just what I needed.

A growing bunch of possible nutcases with bombs.

CHAPTER THIRTY-TWO

On one of my good days, Jess and the others moved much quicker than this old man. The long drive here and sleeping in a strange bed had done nothing to add to that speed. It seemed like every year of the last eight years had added to the pains in my back and knees, slowing me down just a little more.

Halfway up the stairs, and it felt like one of the back-home shopping trips with one of my other granddaughters, the ones where I turned them loose, trailing behind with wallet and moral support.

Already at the top of the stairs before me, Jess interrupted my internal whining with a backhanded tap on the elbow. As the tap brought me to a halt, Jess gave me a nod toward the door Taylor was holding open.

Even then, I had no idea what Jess was going on about. But when she added on the "Were you expecting company?" I got the message.

Sitting on the bench positioned just inside the door was the Norse god who had helped me earlier. He was engaged in a dog petting with a tiny mutt that could not have been more than ten pounds.

Between the size of the dog and the inn's bench, the big guy looked even bigger sitting down. It was if he had added another layer of bulk to an already-powerful mass.

The height of the bench forced the ponytailed warrior to arch his back in order for his elbows to find a resting spot on the knees—a situation that made him look like a fairy-tale giant, the type of figure you found hiding on the side of the road in books, usually waiting for their next human meal to come walking down the road.

Not the best of thoughts, especially when my aching back was making me feel particularly old. At this moment, I would have rather petted a snarling junkyard dog than go through a confrontation, verbal or physical, with this modern-day mammoth.

It crossed my mind to go back down the steps and to our rooms through the lobby. Might be the better part of valor, because if my understanding of the situation was correct, his visit to Mel's had, intentionally or not, led to her demise.

But even if macho pride was supposed to be a thing of the past, I had Jess, Taylor, and Salem with me and did not want to come off as a coward in their eyes.

With that thought in mind, I pressed forward with a smile and a forced nod of my own. In response to my advance, the big guy came to his feet with an ease that shouted of an agility I didn't want to face in a fight.

"Did you see much?"

"Wasn't looking."

"Really." The ice giant edged forward to block my path as he pointed toward the bags in the girls' hands. "Took an awful long time to find a McDonald's located just down the street."

"I took the scenic route."

"And did you see much?"

My full stop was half forced by his position and half intended. I didn't really want a confrontation, but again I was being macho.

Even though the physical anxiety in my gut had skipped past gut-wrenching to a "you got to be kidding" level, I was not going to show any fear in front of my girls.

"Are you watching us?"

"I am watching everybody."

"I don't need a babysitter."

"Neither of us does." The big guy leaned down a bit to give the little dog a pat and seemed to be gathering himself to leave. "But having your back watched in this town is not always a bad thing."

"Really." The tightening in my stomach already forced out the hunger bug and was well into building an acid pit instead. "I have found the locals very friendly."

"The Middle Easterners and your Missouri Christians are not what I consider locals."

"And you?"

He did a head bob that could have almost passed for a bow. "I serve the Mother, just as your son once did."

The Norse giant seemed to be offering a friendship I might need. But then again, could I trust him? There weren't too many defenses against a stab in the back.

Jess took the decision out of my hands.

"You are nothing like my brother."

My daughter came forward to stand by my side with a face showing red, a color to which, when it came out on either of the twins' faces, I found it smarter to avoid any facedown.

"No matter what his religious choice, Junior would never have chased after a mystic evil power to use against the rest of the world."

The giant gave us no comeback but eased a step toward the door before my question held him up.

"Since you seemed to be our shadow, do you have a name?"

"Loki." The towering giant watched my face for a reaction before adding, "An inside joke my mother played on my father."

I wanted to say "Some joke" but held off.

Then it was too late, as with an almost-sad smile, the Wiccan drifted out the door after his mutt.

CHAPTER THIRTY-THREE

I guess after eight years of being away from the local nightmares, I had gotten soft. I figured the least the world owed me was a break for an early dinner, even if it was only made up of rapidly cooling fast food.

I had encouraged Salem and Taylor to make for our room with the food while Jess and I hung back to watch the big guy disappear. I was hoping to pick up the giant's choice of travel but only got him doing a walk through the parking lot and around a corner.

As we ambled toward our room, a couple of curry-smelling men hustled at us from the other side of the tee. They hit the junction right before Jess and me and did a pivot into our section of rooms.

It didn't take a genius to know who they were. When they shifted into bracketing my door, it only confirmed the fact—something I was not sure whether they wanted me to know or not.

Their outfits were an upgrade from the breakfast crowd and porch lurkers. They might have even passed for native-born Americans. But something about them beyond the curry odor still screamed "Middle East terrorists" to any attention-paying profiler at the airport.

We could have just slipped into Jess's room and texted the rest of the team from there or just kept walking to see what the twin troublemakers had in mind but...

At the moment, I was suffering from an overdose of macho.

So two paces short of my room, I came to a halt and nudged my daughter into a partially protected position. Without actually saying a word, I dangled my room key in front of them.

The far guy, who looked to be the more Westernized of the two, twisted to give himself a full view of Jess and me. Then with an accent that would have passed for an East Coast tough guy, he said, "We need your woman with the silver hair."

"No, you don't." I stepped forward to use my key card, holding back just enough to not be between them. "And we have a lunch to eat."

"We heard your companion had long silver hair."

"My daughter is a blond." I moved a little to one side to show them the fact with a long sweeping flourish.

"Four drinks for two people." Neither of the two made a movement to get out of my way. "Perhaps one of the others has silver hair."

"Perhaps we're just thirsty." I gave a dismissive wave to move the guy off to one side. "And the ice is melting and destroying the flavor of our drinks."

I was hoping they would back off with my macho-man approach. But as I reached forward to shove my card key into the slot, a near Arab grabbed my wrist.

"We want the silver-haired girl."

"And I wanted my drink still fresh."

I rolled my weight up on to the balls of my feet and made ready to protect my girls, including, to my surprise, Salem.

"Guess we both lose."

Luckily, my fighting stance was not needed.

The leader of the two reached forward to remove his comrade's hand. His hesitation afterward gave me a chance to fill in a second closer impression of the two.

They were both sporting the brown eyes of the desert. But they were opposites in emotions.

The arm grabber's eyes were blazing hot with nothing resembling friendliness. It didn't take a mind reader to see this guy would have no trouble with the removal of my head with the use of a very sharp sword.

The leader, who had to be older by a few years, probably putting him in his late twenties, had a practiced blank stare—not like he wasn't thinking, but blank like there was nothing there to feel.

I would rather he had hated me and let it show.

It would have been a lot less creepy.

CHAPTER THIRTY-FOUR

We hung like that for a ring around of thoughts, before the leader of the two broke the silence once more.

"We will find the girl!"

"Good luck, but as you can see, we don't have the girl." I leaned forward to insert my key card. "So stay away from our room!"

Neither of them reached out to stop me this time, but getting the door open would have to involve moving one or both of them aside. And the leader was not done with the threats.

"We don't mind hurting old people to find her."

If nothing else, this time, there was a little smoke stealing into the blank eyes. I thought about baiting the smoke into a flame. It shouldn't have been all that hard to manage, but machoism at my age only carries you so far.

I eased back a half-dozen inches and threw my arms out wide to embrace the entire hall and beyond.

"And I don't mind screaming for help." I ignored the muscle half of the duo and jutted my jaw out toward the leader. "And a hallway is an awfully public place to be making such a threat, Khalid."

"Empty hall!"

"Daughter with cell phone." I hooked my shoulder and prayed Jess had her phone out with fingers hovering over the keypad.

"Nobody fears the local police, least of all us."

His eyes transformed back to smoldered black, ice blank. The change made me hope like hell mine were not showing him the drip of cold sweat trickling down my spine.

I felt the pinch in my gut telling me to turn around and head back to Michigan. But I had already gone too far to back down now.

"I didn't say my daughter was going to call the locals."

"Then who?"

That was a great question.

And having an answer would have been just as great.

Without one, I just put on my best "cat that ate the Tweety Bird" grin and hoped it made him stew.

To his credit, his eyes stayed blank, but the face changed around them.

It went to a confident smirk.

Still an ugly look, but one that, for some reason, made me feel a little better. I guess, to my way of thinking, he was human more or less, which in effect gave him weaknesses and made him much easier to attack.

"Why not wait awhile and find out?" *Or hopefully back off now and forever.*

I didn't really want to have to back up my bluff, even with Taylor and the others as possible backup. My girls were not exactly softies, and if my granddaughter caught one of them with her karate kick, they were going down.

Still even with the best of outcomes, somebody on our side would probably get hurt.

Luckily, Omar and Khalid, or whatever their names were, began slithering down the hall. But even then, there was no doubt showing in the lead Arab's eyes. He would have made a great poker player, but his partner, not so much.

He leaned back away from us with his neck muscles straining out to either side and a facial expression showing me all the cards in his deck.

"You might slow Allah's will, but you cannot stop it."

Want to bet?

These dudes hadn't seen me in action against the Father's people on the mountainside.

True, I had been younger and wielding an enchanted battle-ax at the time but pleasingly impressive all the same, at least in my personal memory of the battle.

And if it came to it, I knew in my heart Junior had reached out from the beyond to help, just like he would again this time. Maybe not with an ax transformation like last time, but I knew my son would reach out from the grave to help us once more.

At least I hoped he would.

CHAPTER THIRTY-FIVE

"I t is a lot easier to be brave when they are walking away."

"Them or us?"

"Both?"

I tilted my head to one side and did a partial pivot to get a better view of my daughter's Cheshire cat grin. It cut back on my imaged comeback even before I could get it out. Even trying to flash a return grin seemed kind of lame in comparison to her happiness.

I just wish it could have lasted beyond the opening of the door behind my back. Neither of us had expected Taylor or Salem to be in my room instead of theirs.

Even more surprising was the presence of their guest.

It only took me a three-step dash and a ninety-nine-scary-thought sprint to get inside the door. One or the other sent my heart rate up through the ceiling. What made it even worse, I never got to settle on which of the ninety-nine bad thoughts to bring out before reacting.

"Get out!"

"What are you doing here?"

My questioning wasn't as forceful as Jess's command, but it was delivered in the same overall tone. Unfortunately, we got our biggest reaction from Taylor.

She went up hard and almost jumped out of her jeans getting between us and the woman. But thankfully, the jeans were a good fit and held firmly in place by the belt riding natural on Taylor's hips.

The woman sitting on the edge of the bed behind my grand-daughter was bouncing a familiar toddler on her knee and seemed to expect our verbal attack. Of course, carrying those hateful signs and being yelled at by true Americans had probably given her plenty of practice at hiding any reaction.

Still, without Taylor moving between us, she would have gotten a more physical reaction from me or my daughter, baby bouncing or not.

Jess and I have always been very protective of my granddaughter. Even with Taylor's positioning between us, I was halfway tempted to bypass sex and child to physically remove the pair.

But Taylor was not done.

"She just wants to talk."

Big deal, young lady.

After seeing her group's remodeling of Father's sanctuary, I was even less willing to talk. In fact, in spite of my old-fashioned upbringing, I kind of wished it had been her jaw on the connecting end of the ice bucket.

"Grandpa!"

Taylor must have noticed the clenching of my hands and shifted to get directly between me and the baby bouncer. Her hand also came up to further slow any advance.

But such a move left Jess free to advance.

Seeing this and having to choose between a pair of poor choices, Taylor moved back in front of Jess. Given Taylor's knowledge of her aunt's temper, she knew hitting a bitch was not beyond Jess's behavior, especially this one.

Giving in to Taylor's wish for no harming, I dropped my urge to hit the woman with our ice bucket. Besides, my ice bucket was on the far side of the room and empty.

Because of that, I was left notching my desire down to just a heavy-handed removal from my room.

Slipping past Taylor, I moved forward to do so.

But I didn't get very far as the third member of the group came out of the hotel room's chair. Salem's feline quickness had me gathered into a tight hug before I could think to evade her. From there, I am not sure if it was her body pressed against me or the words whispered into my ear, or maybe both, that halted me.

"Remember, always keep your friends close and..."

CHAPTER THIRTY-SIX

I t wasn't easy, but I forced my fingers out straight.

It took four separate efforts of my part, but in the end, the fists had been replaced by open hands at my side. I only wished I could have done the same with my neck. Those muscles must have stooled out like the cords of a hangman's noose.

I might have been able to crack them loose by rolling my head around, but that would have given away the depths of my feelings. Something I didn't want to do in front of the enemy.

I'm not sure why I cared.

The people in her so-called church did little to hide their feelings from anybody. They seemed to think their beliefs gave them the right to be arrogant and cruel to the rest of the world.

I let myself steal a glance toward my girls and knew there were others more important to please. They needed their leader to stay calm and in charge for their sake.

As if waiting for this cue, the lady greeted the end of my charge by holding out her hand from around the back of the toddlers. And I think she actually expected me to shake it.

"I'm Sarah, from the church of—"

"I know where you are from."

"And our first meeting was…"

"What I should have expected."

Sarah's hand hung there for another few seconds and then withdrew to balance the toddler. The smile lasted a little longer, but not much. She tried to hide the movements by cooing to the baby, but I have been around the proverbial block a few times myself.

I could read the tension in her as well as the next guy.

Better than most.

Ms. Sarah must have figured to do better with Taylor and Salem before my return. Taylor was a teen, and Salem did not look that much older. And neither looked like the ice bucket-swinging type.

In my opinion, she should have stayed working with the toddler.

Taylor was at an age where she doubted everything adult, and Salem, that ageless young lady had survived centuries under the harsh control of the Father and then, in at least some small point, helped engineer his downfall. From what I had seen so far, this woman fell way short of the Father when it came to twisting people around to his way of thinking.

"I just need to talk to you."

"We don't want to listen."

Jess's retort beat me to the gun, but not by much. Just enough to give me a chance to pull back for a microsecond and think over the situation. After all, Salem had pointed out, learning to know your enemy was never a mistake as long as you kept your head about you.

"Talk!"

I held my hand out to clamp down on Jess's tongue.

I knew Jess didn't care for my action any more than I liked making it. But with my hand in her face, Jess was willing to hold back, at least for a moment.

Still I knew, given enough time to stew over Sarah's collection of protest signs, it would take more than an extended hand and a bouncing toddler to save Sarah's ass.

It took a lot to get either of my twins upset, but once there, or to put it best, there were only two people Junior ever admitted to being afraid of. It was a lesson Junior had learned early in life, and it had stayed with him.

Even after Junior had been shipped overseas and suffered a semisteady stream of bullets and rockets being fired in his general direction, Junior held to that one belief like it was fastened to him with gorilla glue.

The big question was knowing my daughter's temperament when it came to disrespecting her brother's memory. I had to wonder if Jess would bother to open the window before throwing our Ms. Sarah out through it.

"We are all Christians on the same side."

Without talking, I dragged my ever-present silver chain out from the top of my shirt.

And then?

I let the last pair of dog tags Junior had ever worn dangle in the air between us.

CHAPTER THIRTY-SEVEN

There were four tags and a religious symbol on Junior's chain.

One of the tags had come to me as a remembrance from Junior's godmother and, unlike the army-issued tags, reflected sunlight like a metal mirror. Since I was standing by the window, it caught more than enough light for such a reflection, which, as luck would have it, went into a twirling gig centered in Sarah's eyes.

Not that it made Sarah any more attractive.

In fact, it made her look worse being in such a sharp contrast to the rest of her looks.

Sarah's clothes were even more shapeless, bland, and offsetting than the outfit she had worn earlier. Add in not so much as a blush to her cheeks and matching brown eyes and hair that showed about as much life as a week-old flattened highway squirrel.

I have to believe a broken pencil lead would have been less boring and probably beaten Sarah in a beauty contest.

"You were in the army?"

"My son was."

"The pagan symbol?"

"Again, my son's."

"And are you pagan as well?"

I rolled the sign of my son's chosen religion into the palm of my hand and closed my finger tightly around it.

I wanted to say yes, as much as anything to drive this bitch up her hate wall, but to do so without joining such a belief seemed like a dishonor to Junior's memory.

So I answered truthfully, "Christian." After all, I did make it across the road to the local church a few times a year, but the visits were far enough apart that I had to add a disclaimer, "More or less."

"Less." Salem moved closer to my side to fold her hands over mine and the emblem. "He sees beyond the dark twisting of what you consider Christian."

I did a soft headbutt with Salem and actually smiled.

"Let's just leave it at 'more or less.'"

"Have you been baptized?" Sarah leaped at a possible opening like a starving leopard and clamped down with fangs and claw when I gave her an agreeing nod. "Then we are on the same side."

Right! If you leaned toward the man on the mountainside preaching to the multitude. Wrong if you sided with the nutcases who twisted their words to burn people at the stake hundreds of years later in Europe.

"Then you know we have to control evil."

Once again, it amazed me how people could take a message of love and understanding and twist it into hate, no matter what the religion.

Every fiber in my being wanted to bark back at Sarah and her belief but went elsewhere to bring myself back under control.

"You should try wiping off your son's drool first."

That comment gave Taylor a chance to sweep in and rescue the little one. Before our Ms. Sarah could react, my granddaughter had the little boy wiped off and sitting with her beside the lifeless TV. A half moment later, she had the tyke chewing on a rapidly cooling french fry.

It made for such a colorful picture I almost hated to bring Sarah back on point. But I did want them out of here as soon as possible. I had already given up the idea of having warm french fries and was hating the idea of cold burgers as well.

"What evil are we talking about?"

"Hers!"

Sarah's eyes bored past me and into Salem with enough hatred for ten people. I almost expected a ray of red hatred to burst out of Sarah's eyes and to burn Salem into a pile of dust.

CHAPTER THIRTY-EIGHT

I had a red burst of my own building up, but instead of letting it blast Sarah, I walled it off, going instead with an unfelt quip.

"I am impressed." I tried gathering up the closest bag of cooling fries to rattle in front of Sarah, hoping she would take the hint and leave. "I didn't realize Salem was important enough to have an evil all her very own."

Sarah didn't take the bag-rattle hint, instead choosing to stomp her foot and roll her eyes.

So I went on with another growled-out comment, hoping Sarah would eventually get tired of listening.

"But then again, I never looked that hard to see if Salem was evil"—I toned it up with a great smart grin—"but since I am a man, Salem could have been fooling me. Women do that to me all the time."

"Her evil is serious."

"Not to me!"

If the windows had been opened, you could have heard Sarah's sigh around the world. But since they were closed, it was trapped with the tension in our room.

In public, I think that would have been Sarah's breaking point.

But she wanted my key to the Witch Rose, and she figured my cooperation would give her Salem.

Sarah was never going to get it, but she was a true believer in her cause. So after a moment of deep prayer and reflection, Sarah took another lesser breath and tried again.

"Your friend here"—Sarah swung a hate motion toward Salem—"controls an ancient evil you cannot begin to image. And one way or another, she is going to lead us to it."

"So you can destroy it?"

"Some evils cannot be destroyed!"

"Then why find it?" I dug into my bag hoping for a hint of warmth but found very little.

"So our church can twist the evil to our sense of good."

The fries were almost as cold as Sarah's voice, and I found my appetite dropping from chilled to frozen.

"That sounds like an awful big task."

"Not for our church, we are the strong and pure of this country."

And puff, there went my appetite for the rest of the week. Without thinking about it, I found the hand drawing out of my fast-food bag, clenched just short of striking fist hard.

"Your church does not know the meaning of the purity of goodness or have the character strength to combat a single petal of the Witch Rose."

Salem's hand flicked past me to pluck away the crumpled bag before it ended up in Sarah's face.

"The Witch Rose would take your hatred and turn it into an ugly evil far beyond your worst nightmare."

"We don't hate."

"The funerals, the signs, the demonstrations?"

"We are doing God's work, and those acts are needed to save this country." Sarah straightened up to add three inches to her indignation while gathering her toddler chest-wise like a pledge to the cross. 'You don't realize our church members are the only ones fighting against the damnation of our country."

"Just like Joe and Adolf."

"Who?"

I wanted to answer Sarah's dumbfounded expression with a "read a book" comeback but figured even spoon-feeding her the answer would not have helped.

For a long hesitation, the room hung in silence except for the giggle of Sarah's toddler. Thinking back, the little guy was probably the only one without a rope of muscles reaching tighter in our spinal cords.

It was Sarah who finally reeled back to her point of view, which, to be truthful, probably made good sense to her.

"Any reasonable person would have to see our need to control her Witch Rose!"

"My son wouldn't have."

"Fags aren't reasonable."

CHAPTER THIRTY-NINE

I didn't know whether to laugh at Sarah for throwing such an out-of-date insult at Junior's memory or simply throw her and the toddler out through the window for the naked intent behind the slur. After everything to be considered had taken a run through my mind, I found myself leaning hard toward a window exit, toddler or not.

Behind me, Taylor had pulped french fries squeezing out between the fingers of her clenched fist, and Jess's eyes had squinted into the slits of an angered lioness. Neither of them would not have made a move to stop me.

But Salem did.

Not physically or with a brilliant statement of wisdom.

Nope, none of that.

Instead, Salem just laughed.

Not with the chuckle of a shared off-colored joke or even the giggle of an embarrassed moment. But with a full-out burst from so deep inside it was about to drag tears out after it.

It was only after Salem had held everyone's complete attention for somewhere over thirty seconds that she broke it off. Before the echo had a chance to die, Salem moved forward with more lunge than step and placed herself instantly in Sarah's personal space.

Salem's following hiss fluttered Sarah's bangs away to either side, and for the first time, I saw a bit of fear in our unwanted guest's eyes.

Then it all came together for me.

Junior a fag?

Yeah, and Mount Rushmore had zebra faces braying out at us instead of presidents. Junior had more than once shown his complete love of the opposite sex.

I couldn't help but let loose of a laugh of my own, which created a new problem for Jess and Taylor. They couldn't decide who to look at: Salem, who had started the confusion, or me, now that I was adding to it.

Finally, I held up my hand and chocked out a "She called Junior a fag!"

It clicked for Jess, and she began a chuckle of her own.

"That might have kept him out of trouble, because liking women sure didn't."

The chuckle switched toward a hearty laugh, and Taylor's eyes did a mind jump.

"My mother was not trouble."

"According to the army, officially she was for both of them."

I couldn't stop my head shaking, and Jess had to hold her sides in place before blurting out her next thought. It was the revelation everyone concerned had been dancing around for over eight years.

"Your dad, Junior, once he got out of high school, never really pushed that hard for sex." With the first part said, it took a hesitation for Jess to go on. But with another breath under her belt, Jess brought the rest of her thought out with a rush of words. "So of course, all the girls came on to him like a tropical rainstorm, hot and torrid."

Taylor's blush went two shades beyond scarlet as the thought of her father having sex hit her. True, she had never gotten to meet him. Still, fathers did not have sex; that was reserved for kids.

And then Taylor looked across the room at Sarah's entirely confused expression.

I am not sure which one hit Taylor the hardest.

But I do know one or both plucked out her grin, and then Taylor was suddenly laughing with the rest of us nutcases. Within a blink of Taylor's teenage discovery of adult humor, we had three laughers fighting off the blindness of saltwater tears and one cat lady glaring down at the confused nutcase.

When you put it all together, it was more than a mere mortal nutcase could endure.

Sarah slipped under Salem's space intrusion and made a run for the doorway with a french fry-clutching toddler bouncing against her chest.

I, for one, was overjoyed with Sarah's retreat.

I just wished her flight had come before our food had gotten cold.

CHAPTER FORTY

No one except Salem had any interest in cold burgers and heatless fries.

After her recent road trip to Michigan, anything with a classification about cat food and garbage rated as high-end dining. But to the rest of us, eating reheated fast food warmed in the room's microwave seemed just above as appetizing as the cat food.

So in the end, we overrode Salem's protest about exposure and made another trip to the downstairs café. But that seemed like less of a good idea when I spotted our friendly bellboy.

He was off to one side of the lobby and ducking back out of the way, obviously erasing any sight line to the desk clerk as he was apparently struck by a sudden need to make a cell phone call, all the while staring hard in our direction.

I couldn't be 100 percent sure, but odds were high that phone call was not of benefit to our party. I came to a full stop and hesitated with thoughts of murderous mayhem in mind—you know, the ones leading to the breaking of a few or all of his bones. Or better yet, I could leave him to Taylor's gentle karate touch after telling her about how this particular bellboy had affected Salem's safety.

I am sure Taylor would leave him with some unforgettable memories and a long history of therapy for a crushed macho image. But while I hated to admit it, that might have been carrying revenge a bit too far.

But sooner to later, I was going to make this kid pay for his actions. And at least for now, I could savor the possibilities throughout our meal.

Or so I thought.

Taylor came back to drag me into the café toward a window-side table, the one where Jess and Salem were already in place with a full array of place settings and water.

We were almost across the room and within chair-grabbing range when I realized there were more than four settings on the table. The extra one seemed to be for the person to Jess's right. It took me a moment longer, two more steps, and his half turn to recognize the extra.

It was the old man from Mel's.

My right hand might have found the back of the chair but seemingly forgot how to pull it back away from the table. It was as if my mind was frozen in a switch of interest from bellboy to retired police detective.

This whole situation was becoming all too much like a video game, one where we were making our way through an evil city and I was having trouble telling the good guys from the bad, or, for that matter, the innocent bystanders.

Why shouldn't this geezer eat here?

It was a cheap-enough place for a retired city worker to frequent. And we were well within established eating time, and he was a lifetime resident of the town, or so he claimed.

"Detective Green-Jeans was just finishing his lunch." Jess slid her chair over to give me some extra room. "And seeing us entering, he decided to stick around and visit."

"Retired detective Green-Jeans"—our unwanted guest broke out his retired-old-man smile while he gauged my mood with his eyes—"I am glad to join you, but if I am intruding, I can leave."

I glanced around my trio and saw neither confirmation nor denial. For the first time ever, all three of the ladies were interested in various far parts of the room with not an eye available to meet mine.

It was nice of them to leave me to choose between rudeness and polite acceptance. Either way, I would choose wrong, and the girls would be glad to correct me later.

Keeping my sigh inside and out of sight, I forced out a fake smile and motioned for him to stay in place.

"You're not intruding, but in all fairness, I have to warn you, this has not been the best of days, and you might find us all in a creeped-out mood."

Green-Jeans widened his grin to show a bit of tooth with a bit of added chuckle. "Probably our small town getting to you. It has that effect on big-city folk coming here from Michigan."

Hemlock made this city look like a major metropolis, and on top of that, I lived several miles outside Hemlock proper. But since we sometimes used Saginaw as a focal point for our location, maybe Green-Jeans had relied on that. Or even more likely, he figured everyone in Michigan came from Detroit.

Only I could not remember if I had given any of that information to Green-Jeans. But even if I hadn't, Jess might have mentioned it before my arrival.

So I forgot about it for the moment.

Chapter Forty-One

"More the inn then the town itself."

I flashed a grin around the table, making sure every one of my girls saw I was trying to be nice. But I am sure at least Jess knew being nice was getting harder by the minute, but I kept trying.

"I'm just not used to this many strangers going out of their way to talk to me."

I saw the mischief in Jess's eyes even before the words came out. "Most people with any common sense avoid talking to my dad."

"Really!"

The detective turned all his attention on Jess and oozed a well-practiced charm into his next words, "I find that hard to believe. Your father seems like a very nice man to me."

Both Taylor and I could have told Green-Jeans his efforts at charm were a waste of time. Jess didn't charm easy; in fact, I am not sure she charmed at all. At work and home, Jess was generally the one in command, except with me.

And even then, at times, it seemed to be more hope than reality on my side.

Before I mused more on my daughter's personality, Taylor placed her menu to the right of her setting so she could join her aunt in the old-man-put-down session.

"My friends call my grandfather the grumpy old man." As the words came out, Taylor made sure to add on the side an eye blink only I could see as if to silently add, "But they also call him grandpa and seem to love carrying on conversations with him."

I flicked my sight line to Salem, waiting for her to join in on old-man bashing, but I saw no sign of it in her face.

There was neither the smile nor frown I had expected in Salem's expression but something else entirely. If I had been younger and more confident in my macho appeal, I might have mistaken Salem's look for an encouragement.

"Your grandfather told me you knew Mel."

"Yes, sir." Taylor's smile ran away, and I, for one, got ready for some tears. "Better than most."

"You were very young back then."

Okay, just one tear and you, Detective Green-Jeans, were leaving. But to my surprise, the tears did not come, just a lot of tightening in her voice as Taylor explained further.

"She was my first grandparent."

"But..."

The retired detective never got any further as Taylor jammed her hand out between them. "Mel adopted me with affection and more kindness than any little girl could expect."

"I can understand that." The old man leaned so far back in his chair that the front legs almost came off the ground. From there, Green-Jeans beamed out what he probably considered a grandfatherly look of his own. "Mel was such a lovely old lady. She always greeted everyone with those great big smiles of hers."

Taylor twitched out the smallest of grimaces before lapsing into silence. The rest of the table might have followed her example, but a waitress we had never met before came over to take our orders. By the time the last of our orders had been scribbled down, Taylor had drifted back to more or less normal.

Unfortunately, Detective Green-Jeans was still at our table to disturb my mood. I didn't really care for him even if everyone else seemed to accept his presence.

"Anything I can do to help brighten your mood?"

"Only if you know someone renting rooms by the day."

I should have held back that quip, but it had been a long day. And it actually shut down the retired detective Green-Jeans for a long moment. The old guy sat there with his head dropped down in complete concentration as he fingered the silverware of his setting around the glass and napkin a half-dozen times.

"Not a room." Green-Jeans brought the last of his coffee up toward his lips, hesitating a half inch short to add, "But I used to hunt and I have a cabin just a few miles outside of town that could be rented out."

"How far out of town?"

Jess reacted first, but I followed her lead enough to lean into Green-Jeans's answer.

"A fifteen-minute drive if you take the new road, less if you speed a bit"—retired detective Green-Jeans place his drained coffee cup back directly in the center of his place mat—"and very secluded."

I chewed at the inside of my lip as I checked around the table for clues to the girls' position on the offers. I got a small nod from Jess and an even tinier agreement from Salem, but my granddaughter's reaction was different.

She seemed to be doing a bit of lip chewing of her own.

In my own mind, there seemed to be a distant echo of a bell ringing out an alarm.

But why?

Because of my long day?

It had already shown a perchance for people willing to help my problem, as long as it matched their own goals.

Was Detective Green-Jeans any different?

He was a local.

People around here had little love for the Father and his cult. And from what I had seen so far, these newcomers were no better liked. The unasked-for aid from the waitress and staff this morning had confirmed as much.

Detective Green-Jeans was probably cut from the same material, and besides, I really didn't want to stay in the inn, at least not with our overfriendly bellhop spying on us.

I caught another firmer nod from Salem, and the decision was made.

"How much?"

"Fifty dollars a day to cover utilities and the cost of opening it up."

The retired detective had answered more to his coffee cup than me. Perhaps he was afraid the price was a little steep, but it was a lot less than our combined rooms in the inn.

I agreed to pay for a three-day stay in advance, adding on further days in threes as well. Green-Jeans's thank-you was nice, but the look in his eyes was even nicer.

We took to our meals with a gusto that had largely been missing since our arrival, aided more by our mood than the taste of the food.

It just felt good to trust someone again.

CHAPTER FORTY-TWO

We went at our food in relative silence after retired detective Green-Jeans left our table. He was headed out to make arrangements for the opening of his cabin, and personally, I didn't miss his presence.

Two of my tablemates and I promptly went into quiet mode because of the combination of hunger and fatigue. We were too busy shoveling in the food like hungry dogs, with one gobbled bite quickly followed by the next.

Only the young lady to my left seemed less than 1 percent interested in eating.

Out of the corner of my eye, I watched the young cat loose a small bite of hot beef sandwich, freeing it up for a downward stab by her fork. Then the morsel got a drive through the plate for an added layer of gravy before finally coming away from the place setting for an upward soar toward her waiting mouth.

Only unlike the similar movements the rest of us were using, hers were dragged out in super slo-mo, and once the bite reached stuff in mouth position, it hung there, being examined like an ugly bug dragged up from the bottom of a septic tank.

Instead of running first to the dessert section, or at least a close second, my girl didn't finish at all. She took almost three quarters of the sandwich with her in a leftover container and was a hard pass on the after-meal sweet offerings.

Leaving the café, I hung back to give our something-off lady, a chance to spill the beans away from the other two. But before I could whisper a "What's up," we turned into the lobby and smacked into a hurrying bellboy.

Not sure where the kid was going, but I was now blocking his path. And with my two ladies just far enough in front and to either side, we formed an arch around the snitch.

Even if unplanned, we had effectively trapped the bellboy into a confrontation. Before he could back up, I brought my hands up to get his attention.

"Can I help you, sir?"

"Doubtful."

The boy tilted his head to one side as I grinned.

"I think we both know you have been helping more than enough people already."

"Sir"—a flicker of doubt cast a shadow deep in the bellboy's hazel eyes, but his smile still read smug—"did I miss something?"

"You didn't miss a thing."

Smug was beginning to slip.

And being me, I didn't mind nudging it a bit more.

I didn't really mind, until the punk was realizing something was up, and the smug wafted toward skull face. Locking it there, after a hesitation for effect, I added, "You started selling the information about us to some un-nice people."

The boy tried to back away, but Jess shifted to block his retreat. Then Jess rocked forward to give the kid a chest bump when he tried to slip through the opening between her and me.

A glance the other way showed the boy the eyes of the predator cat framed by Salem's silver hair. And it didn't take a genius to realize, even with the desk only a few yards away, he was in serious peril.

Now the eyes coming back to me were pleading, "Don't hurt me," which was even further accented by a strong odor emitting from just a few inches below his beltline.

"Because of that, I am going to give the best tip you are ever going to get."

The tiny flash of greed running through the boy's eyes told me all I needed to know about the kid.

So I finished our conversation.

"Our stay here is up in three days, and then we are heading south for our final destination." I reached out to gather in the boy's shoulder with a less-than-soft grip. "If by some chance that information is leaked and we find somebody waiting or if we are followed, I promise you, I will come back here to get you fired and likely in need of a hospital visit."

"Sir, you can't hit me. I am just a kid."

"I might not be able, but my girls, especially the youngest one, would be able to get away with it. And I know they would love doing it."

CHAPTER FORTY-THREE

We left the kid behind us in the lobby to chew over my threats, while our party retreated back to our floor and into Jess and Taylor's room.

I held back like a gentleman to let the ladies go first, a move I also hoped would buy me a little time, but it didn't. With my first step beyond the closing door, I found Jess pivoting into my face.

"Giving information to the other side?"

"Glad you approved."

"Approved?"

Jess couldn't decide whether to address her next comment to me or our cat girl, Salem, who had jumped into our conversation with her one-word question.

Only Taylor wanted to stay uninvolved for reasons of her own.

In the end, my half-assed grin won out over Salem's puzzlement. Jess's look settled completely on me as she went back to the interrogation.

"You think fear is going to beat out greed?"

"I hope not!"

"You hope not?"

"Yep?"

Jess's mouth opened again, but before her next words came out, Jess's jaws did a slow clamp.

To my other side, Salem's expression slipped into the "know-it-all grin" you often saw on cats. It seemed what I had said in the lobby was finally being redigested.

"You told him three days." Jess glided backward to the edge of her bed and sank into it. "And we're planning on slipping away tonight after everything shuts down."

My self-satisfied nod was cut short as Salem jumped in to pose the negative, "At least one of more of the groups will still be checking the parking lot and notice our absence."

"Probably, but the kid won't be checking!" I put a finger-point exclamation point on it. "I don't see him as really that bright."

"The other groups?"

"It should take them awhile to pick up on the missing vehicles and give us some escaping room."

Or so I hoped.

"Your ruse might work even better if we left one of the vehicle, and"—Jess put a thumb under her jaw with an accompanying finger resting between upper lip and nose—"since the rooms are already paid for, a Do Not Disturb sign should keep out the cleaners."

Salem slipped over to take up a standing position next to Jess's bed and out of my reach.

"Can't hurt."

Yes, it can.

Four people in one vehicle meant Jess's ride and not mine.

Unless, of course, I could talk Salem and Taylor into riding in the bed of my Ranger. And even if I got them to buy into the idea, I couldn't see it happening.

The last thing we needed was to be stopped by a bored third-shift police officer with nothing much to do. Arresting two girls riding unbuckled in the back of my Ranger would give him chuckles with the precinct for weeks.

"Good idea." I doubt if there was much joy in my agreement, and even less when I added on, "And maybe you girls should all sleep over here tonight, so I can get a good sleep before leaving my Ranger behind."

"That bad?"

"Worse!" Taylor came alive to answer Salem. "To Grandpa, that Ranger is his key to personal freedom."

I hated it when my kids were smarter than me.

Since we wanted to clear the hotel parking lot before it came alive, we were planning a super early departure. I used an early bedtime as an excuse to back away.

Still hurting, I gave them each a personalized good evening and edged out of the room. But I could not make a clean getaway because of the urchin inching out behind me.

"Grandpa." Taylor pulled the door behind her within an inch of being shut then dragged her eyes up from the floor to meet mine. "Do you remember Mel being motherly?"

"To you."

Taylor bobbed an agreement but added a clarifier, "But most people?"

I had only eaten there a few times, and I really liked the lady. Mel was great to people she liked and civil in her own way to most others. But I had to admit, Mel was downright rude to the people she didn't like for one reason or another.

"Motherly"—I twisted my jaw around to tilt my face into a half grimace—"would be stretching it."

Still maintaining a grip on the door handle, Taylor reached out to give me a one-handed hug and kiss on the cheek and then a final word as she retreated into her room.

"Just what I was thinking."

CHAPTER FORTY-FOUR

"**W**ake up, Dad."

That wasn't going to happen, unless my daughter had a blow horn and a gallon of cold water to throw at me.

Instead of dozing off last night as I had promised the girls, I paced the room. I had tried watching various odds and ends on the provided television channels, but everything was about as interesting as a snail race using just the shells. Even lying down didn't last more than a few minutes at best.

I shouldn't have been like this.

It wouldn't be the first time I had left my Ranger behind. Hell, it had sat in the Flint Airport for a couple of weeks at a time.

But this time, it felt wrong.

This community had almost eaten me up once before, and it hadn't changed all that much since then. If nothing else, having the Ranger close by gave me connection with my real world where small children were not fed to a killer plant just for a few years' extension of our own.

Three times between nine and one, I had snuck down to sit in my Ranger and reconsider our plans for the next few days. It seemed to me, maybe turning around for home was, as they say, "the better part of valor."

The last time down, I even thought of leaving the kids a note and going home by myself. The only thing worse than the growing apprehension building a temple in my gut was the even deeper fear of letting Taylor, Jess, and Salem down. Finally, I dozed, but not hard enough to clear my mind.

It kept drifting back over my last trip to the mountainside with dreams so real I actually shivered from the downfall of the cold rain.

I was in a sleepy midrecall when I got a pillowed jolt in the side of my face. One would have been bad enough, but it was followed at once by a second, third, and finally, a rapid series of jolts. Each one gathered more force as the body at the end of my bed added another bounce.

"Come on, Dad." The all-too-familiar voice came at me again from the end of the bed. "Time to get up."

Thinking about it, the voice was longtime familiar, but not quite right for my daughter across the hall. And forcing myself up on my elbow gave me a glimpse of the wrong hairdo.

At least for Jess, but not for her sister, Jody.

But since Jody was back in Michigan, the whole setup with Salem must have been a dream.

I found a smile registering, but then I got a look at the room around me.

It wasn't mine.

That got me rolling around into a sitting position.

"You're not supposed to be here."

"Really!" Jody broke out an ear-to-ear grin. "My sister seemed to feel otherwise."

"When?"

"Yesterday, when you began talking about sneaking away from the inn for your assault on the Witch Rose." Jody's grin was now a thing of the past. "I was already loaded and on the road before Jess called back to confirm the move."

"Didn't I tell you stay home?"

"I thought that was for Jess, in order to keep Taylor out of it." Jody did her head twist to search out a far corner of the room, the one she used to avoid my eyes when making a questionable point. "So technically, Jess is the one who didn't listen, and I am just Lone Ranger riding to the rescue."

"You don't say." Jody's grin came back toward me even broader than before. "And where is Tonto?"

"In the back under a scattering of blankets so the cases don't show."

I wasn't surprised.

I had come home with the memory of how guns failed to work within a certain distance of the Witch Rose. And since I wasn't planning on a shoot-out in town, there didn't seem much use for bringing any.

On the other hand, if you went deep down inside, neither of my twins completely believed my story from the mountainside. An old war ax and enemies shimmering away into nothingness was Junior's world, not theirs.

"My forty-forty?"

"And your two seventy." Jody's expression was life-and-death serious. "Also Jess and mine's personal protection with a selection of long guns just in case."

Personally, I didn't see guns helping us on the mountainside, but if it made the girls feel better, they were not a complete waste.

And you never knew.

CHAPTER FORTY-FIVE

By the time I finished my wake-up shower, the girls had everything loaded in Jody's SUV. According to them, the entire time of their loading, they had seen only a single late arriving guest use the parking lot and, after registering, had left their car nestled up close to the office.

Even the streets were vacated.

You would have thought we were staying out west in a ghost town, making the lack of traffic even more apparent.

During our entire-mile-and-a-quarter trip to the far side of the town, we saw only three signs of life: a couple of semitrucks going past us in the other direction and a police car that was parked and running for paperwork completion or an on-duty nap.

Back at the hotel, Jody had pushed hard for me sharing the Ranger with Salem. She claimed a need to catch up with her twin, even though they had only been apart a few days and (I now knew) had been in phone contact.

Going on past experience?

Instead of catching up, I figured my twins were comparing notes on either their dad, Salem, or Taylor. Since Taylor was sharing their ride and Salem was new to our family, the odds were super high in favor of me being their conversational target.

We found retired detective Green-Jeans waiting for us at the abandoned gas station on the edge of town. Its modernized replacement was just across the street, and while its glowing lights chased off the worse of the darkness, the station was closed for the night and unmanned.

Still parked as we were, with the station's glow and the moon-light combined, you could barely make out the facial expressions of the ones sharing our meeting. From what I could see of their body language, this meeting was not going all that encouraging.

Neither Salem nor Taylor bothered getting out of their rides, and Jody seemed to have lost her tongue since waking me up. And even though Jess took part, she didn't add all that much to the conversation.

In the end, I finalized the last of the details with the retired detective and handed over the cash to give us temporary control of his cabin. In return, Green-Jeans furnished me with a set of keys and a pair of roughly drawn maps to the cabin. According to Green-Jeans, we shouldn't need them, but the turnoff and farther outlets down the pathway would look different in the daylight.

I guess he figured better safe than lost.

Then to top off my early morning journey, I got the dubious honor of riding with the detective to the cabin.

Green-Jeans tried to talk my ear off.

He went into great detail about his long-standing friendship with Mel while at the same time doing his best with interjected questions to draw out information about my last trip up the mountain.

And while the retired detective might not have been the last person I was telling about that night, he was up there close to the top.

Finally, I had to tell Green-Jeans I needed my complete attention on the roadside. I pointed out to the blabbermouth how I might need to pick out some landmarks, explaining it was just in case we needed supplies or more intel from the city.

To be honest, there weren't many to pick out.

One growth of trees looked just like the next, and the few breaks that I saw were all grassy covered fields. There were a couple of road-side billboards and a lot of twists and turns, but nothing that seemed to stand out in any way.

It was sheer luck I found a dead tree standing by itself in a small clearing. Close enough to the road-side, I was able to make it out in the moon-light, and it was definitely one of a kind, gargled and weathered from a lifetime plus of guarding the west-side entrance to the mountain pass.

It might not have been the biggest dead tree in the forest, but it was everything we needed. And it stood in direct sequence with Green-Jeans's use of his blinker and the beginning of his slowdown.

A hundred yards farther on, Green-Jeans was making his turn on to a well-kept gravel road.

The tree would probably be an even better marker in the full light of the day.

As Green-Jeans made his turn off the highway, I glanced back to double-check the rest of our convoy.

My daughter Jess was driving close enough to follow our taillights into the turn, while my other daughter, Jody, sported less than a truck length between my Ranger and her.

I was surprised she wasn't closer.

Jody was one of the best drivers I knew, but slow and careful was not in her genes. Riding with her was an adventure. It kept my foot firmly planted on the floorboard, braking for my daughter from the passenger side.

My braking must have worked because I was still alive.

Once into the turn, the pathway was more or less straight. Except for a few turnoffs, usually coming as a split in the road, I figured the other paths led toward other homes or hunting cabins. We passed them all, taking the right-hand split leading up deeper into the mountain.

I probably should have questioned my guide better, but I couldn't handle much more of Green-Jeans's yammering. Maybe it was from a lack of sleep, but there was just something about it that grated on my nerves.

Finally, we pulled into a driveway leading off to the right.

It seemed a bit more used than a pathway for a deer-hunting cabin. Detective Green-Jeans's explanation was a claim of use as a turnaround by the various maintaining crews who worked out here.

His claim rang false, but I was too tired and irritable to question it further. After my trip out here, I would have probably doubted my driver if Green-Jeans had claimed the sun would be coming up in the East.

There wasn't time to check out the cabin details as Green-Jeans pulled to a stop in front of the cabin. There for the first time of our trip, Green-Jeans put on a somber look as he twisted the keys to turn off the car.

"One request."

The question held up my reach for the door handle, hanging my hand midair until the detective finished.

"Please respect my privacy and stay out of the bedroom drawers and closet. They hold my late wife's things."

Chapter Forty-Six

I watched our detective Green-Jeans drive out of sight thinking retired police officers got their picks of nice rides. It was a thought quickly pushed away by the more important thought of whether I should settle for the sofa or claim one of the two bedrooms. I was so engrossed I didn't realize I had company. At least not until Jody's arm locked into a crook of my left elbow.

"You have always believed Junior was watching over us."

"Don't you?"

"Not like you."

Jody tightened her hold and leaned against my shoulder.

It seemed like forever, or at least since I had read a story by Robert E. Howard about Conan the Barbarian. In it, Conan's true love had refused to allow death to stop her from coming back to protect Conan in his time of need.

It was a nice-enough idea; one I could take to heart, but not one I could completely believe in.

At least not until the first time I held a pair of little ladies in my arms and they blessed me with a pair of matching smiles. After that, each time I rocked one or both of my twins, I knew if my kids ever needed me, I would come back from the gates of hell itself to protect them.

Junior's follow-up birth a few years later only strengthened my belief.

Of my trio, Junior was the one who took my belief to heart. He actually gave us the same promise as he got ready to leave for his deployment.

"I will watch over you from beyond the grave and be there if you need me."

And now?

"At times, Jess and I actually think you believe your story about what happened here."

"I do!" I twisted to see Jody as I talked, loosening her hold to a gripless one. "It's the truth."

"Dad?"

As Jody turned to face me head-on, she let her arm slide away until only a hand was left in the crook of my elbow. She didn't need much more, as her eyes locked into mine with a seriousness I had only seen twice before.

I hadn't liked it any better back then.

"You suddenly find an ancient war ax in your hand that turns people into fairy dust?" Jody's words were accompanied by the barest hint of headshake with more to come. "Even Sandy and John doubted your story."

"They didn't that night."

"Agreed." Jody retightened her grip on my elbow. "Maybe not that night, but when they got away from the stress of it all, they began comparing what they saw to reality."

"And Taylor?"

"She was hardly more than a baby." Jody's grip notched up into a heavy pinch. "Even now Taylor refuses to doubt you."

Aww.

So their drive from the inn to the station had been a lead up to this. It brought up a lot of doubts to the strength of our relationships.

But at least one of my brood had not felt the same.

"So you think I lied?"

"You fantasized, and it helped you accept Junior's death just a little bit better." Jody's eyes softened, and her grip loosened all the way to gentle. "And that was a good thing."

"And Salem switching from cat to human."

"Have you ever seen it happen?"

Results?

Yes.

The actual event?

No.

For a second, I blinked.

Was I so old that I imaged the whole thing to make up for the loss of my son?

I had seen my aunt lose touch with reality, but it had been a gradual thing caused by old age and dementia. Yet once started, the downward spiral just kept getting worse until, in the end, she didn't know her own family.

But the blink ended with a familiar sense of a touch felt years before on this same mountain. It wasn't a heaviness weighing me down but rather to-lift-me-up touch. It gave me the knowledge that I wasn't alone and Junior would be with me later if I needed him.

I only had to keep believing in the love of a son for his family.

CHAPTER FORTY-SEVEN

Before our conversation could go any further, an electrified shot of yellowed brightness hit us from the direction of the town. Two blinks later, the flash was followed by an oppressive grinding of air roared into our ears.

I didn't want to think about it.

If I was even halfway right, it was the last thing I needed right now.

But as per usual, I couldn't control my thinking—or my daughter's mind, for that matter, who must have been thinking with the same mind, only with younger reflexes.

"Another gas explosion?"

I gave Jody a look that said, "You had to ask?"

She shrugged back as the next question came from the doorway.

"An accident?"

"A something."

I sent the answer to Jess as she joined us at the edge of the porch. We spent a couple of held breaths watching the new light flicker up from the area of the flash. Then one my twins turned to the other with less-than-happy expressions.

"The inn?"

"The flash was too far over." That brought out another exchange of twin looks, but I cut them off before they could ask. "I'll tell you when I get back."

"Dad! You're not."

"I am!"

I didn't wait for more but went into the cabin to gather up my keys. Only they were no longer on the table where Jody had left them. And before I could start back to get them from my daughter, the Ranger's horn broke the silence.

I dropped my shoulder and looked up past my brow to the ceiling for any help from above.

It didn't come.

Instead, I dragged myself out to my Ranger without the slightest chance of any surprise, because, as expected, I found Taylor in the passenger seat with a large silver cat on her lap.

"Any chance?"

No words, just a dangling of the keys out the far window.

In response, I slipped behind the wheel and held out my hand for the keys. Taylor brought them in and, with the decor of a teenager getting her way, centered the keys into the absolute middle of my palm.

"Cat?"

"The Ranger only has two seats." And Salem would be harder to spot in her reduced size, but Taylor skipped that fact.

Once back in town, the flickering in the sky was easy to follow. It led back to a familiar neighborhood and a building I knew oh so well.

Tonight, we couldn't get right up to the building. The police had set up blockades forcing us to park almost three blocks away, and even our walking was halted two blocks later.

From there, I had a pretty good view of the building where Father had headquartered his cult. But it didn't look like it would ever headquarter anything ever again.

From what I could see, the building was pretty well gutted with a melody of flames dancing the length of the structure. Even the firemen seemed to know there was no saving anything. It looked as if they were only half-heartedly fighting the fire, concerning themselves instead more with the prevention of it spreading to other neighboring lots.

What was more troubling to me was the scene kitty-corner to me, where our Detective Green-Jeans was exchanging words with another pair of men: one I knew as our giant, Loki from the inn, while the other seemed to be a matching version, only with more years riding on his shoulders.

From my location, I couldn't hear anything spoken over the noise around me, but their body language spoke volumes.

While the older pagan seemed bored, Loki and retired detective Green-Jeans were giving off an air that was less than agreeable. I almost expected the big guy to rip Green-Jeans's head off and throw it in my direction.

Fearing the discovery of our presence, I nudged Taylor and edged back toward our ride, a trip that would have gone faster if not for Taylor's apprehension about Salem, who had slipped away from us during our approach.

I whispered for her not to worry, and like a prophet from the ages, I was right.

We found Salem waiting by the Ranger, and I was about to open the door for the waiting feline when a voice from behind caught up to us.

"Interesting cat."

CHAPTER FORTY-EIGHT

Driving back toward the cabin, I could not work my mind off the giant we had left behind on the sidewalk.

I had no real proof of the evil intent.

But finding the older pagan creeping up on my Ranger felt a bit too ominous. It might have been just bad luck, but the timing? I had to believe we had been spotted out of the corner of an eye and followed.

I imagine the old guy had to be the father of our pagan from the inn. They had the look of close relations.

Of course, the old man was an inch or so shorter than his son, but he had the same long hair, only the older pagan had a thick scattering of gray mixed in. Their facial features were definitely a close match, and if you took away a few pounds of old age, the body shape would have been identical.

The only real difference was not a visual feature.

It was more a sense of being.

Loki, our giant pagan from the inn, came across as caring and helpful in his own way. Even if it was an act to gain our trust, it was hard to dislike Loki.

No such problem with the elder version.

He carried no such positive vibe.

Instead, he cast a sinister cloud worse than the bombing over our night. With just two words, the old guy had ripped a pit so deep in my gut it left my spine more jelly than bone. In retrospect, making our trip to the explosion site seemed worse than a bad idea.

"Think he knew?"

We were off the highway and on our dirt road by the time Taylor finally broke the silence. And her question didn't really need an answer, but I gave it a delayed nod just the same.

"He spooked Salem."

I slowed down to just short of a stop to free my eyes for a sideways glance. I didn't see where Salem was shaking or looking especially shaken up, but it was hard to tell with a cat. I had never known them to show much of anything except for disdain and a show of complete superiority.

"She buried her head against my hip and hasn't lifted it to give me a single look"—okay, that did not seem like Salem, and even less so when Taylor added—"or move away from my petting."

Now I did come to a stop to study Salem.

It took a full thirty seconds for Salem to acknowledge my attention. And then it was only with a blinking of the eyes and the slightest of a head lift.

But she was not so listless when we reached the cabin.

She was squeezing out the door and headed for the back side of the cabin long before Taylor got the Ranger's door more than a fourth of the way open. You would have thought there was a whole pack of huge dogs munching on her tail, literally.

Of course, my twins standing together in the harsh glare of the Ranger's headlights almost had me doing the same. Neither of the girls seemed glad to see me, and I suddenly realized fatigue brought a third member on to their side. And shutting off my headlights did little to wash the rigorousness of their stance.

"Did you think we could go back to town without paying for it later?"

The words came from Taylor, still maintaining an iron grip on her door. I think we both knew she wasn't kidding.

"Only if we stay there for the rest of our lives."

After my answer, we shared a look and dual sighs. Taylor and I swung out of our respective doors of the Ranger and began a walk over to the twins. It was more of a death march than "glad you're back" stroll.

"Dad!"

Crap, they were even greeting me in unison. They hadn't done that since I threatened to explain education to Taylor's misguided principal.

From there, I think Jody was going to take the lead in a dual assault, but I was saved by Salem's hurried return. It came with a gauntness, which, for the first time ever, showed a hint of her real age.

"Bad?"

"They're all dead."

"No chance of the children surviving?"

Taylor's question was more squeal then words.

"Not if they were in the building." Salem's eyes swept through us all while settling on none. "There is nothing left of Father's hell den. It is just gone from three feet up and beyond, with the houses across the street showing a heavy pelting from the debris and a lot of damage to their roofs and siding."

"Dad!"

This time, it was Jess taking the lead, but I didn't care.

All I could think of was a toddler and the other children, the ones we had seen during my earlier passing by.

They were too young to be involved in this, yet somehow, once again, innocence with their whole life in front of them had become victims of the Witch Rose.

With that in mind, I was just too tired to think about anything.

"We have to talk!"

"Later, we need some sleep."

"Now, Dad." Jody had retaken the lead, but Jess was jutting her jaw forward in hard agreement.

"Later!"

The severity in my voice shocked even me, but I didn't care. I needed to get inside and away from children dying all too early.

And for once, my daughters knew better than to try to stop me.

CHAPTER FORTY-NINE

I was tired, dragged out, and emotionally shot.

But I knew I had too much on my mind to sleep.

Still, somehow, the next thing I remember after stretching out on the couch was the sun outside. It was reaching for the high point of the day.

The second thing to catch my eye took longer to review. I couldn't help but take in a full measure of the silver goddess sharing my morning. Apparently, she had watched over the last moments of my sleep.

"Four hours?"

"Over six."

I must have been tired, but even with six hours under my belt, the body still wanted more. When I finally worked up into a sitting position, it took a neck twisting to either side, accompanied, of course, by several Rice Krispies—Snaps, Crackles, and Pops—to get any freedom of movement back, which was a good thing.

It gave me a great view of my guardian's stretching rise from her chair. And while the body was a woman's, the stretch was all feline.

About halfway up, Salem caught my stare and added a smile, one that was all woman and all-knowing.

"Now, are you ready for some hell?"

"From?"

"A pair of concerned daughters."

I closed my eyes and tried to chase the morning away, but no matter how tight I kept them, reality was forcing its way in with the force of a jackhammer. But it did get a little better when a surprisingly gentle hand landed on my shoulder to kneed at the tightness.

It was a human touch I had missed without realizing it. It was both relaxing and arousing at the same time. I found it easy to mentally hope for a long application.

But it didn't come.

Instead, I got a final squeeze as Salem's hand came off my shoulder, only to join its counterpart in reaching down to gather in my hands for a tug off the couch.

She held to my right hand all the way to the porch-side council waiting my arrival. None of the three looked at ease, with Taylor being the most stressed of the trio.

"Green-Jeans lied to us."

"You expected the truth?"

"About owning this cabin." Jody's indignation was even sharper than Jess's, bringing the last word come out like a thunderclap. "Yes!"

"That might actually be the truth."

With that settled, I plunked myself down on the edge of the porch. It was just high enough to let my feet reach the ground flat-footed. Actually, a quite comfortable place to sit until Taylor dropped a framed picture into my lap.

The picture was a photo of an elderly couple sitting about two feet to the left from where I was sitting at the moment. Only the weather was colder with the need for a heavy layer of clothing.

They looked like they belonged together.

"I found it in the locked closet."

"*Locked* means 'to stay out.'"

"I'm a teenager." Taylor grabbed the railing and swung down next to me. "We consider *locked* an invitation."

I gave Taylor a sideways glance and reminded myself to get some better locks when we got back home. Then I made to give the picture back to her when Jody got back into the action.

"Dad!"

Okay.

I had heard several tones of serious over the years, but with Jody, this was a new one. It had more depth and fear than ever before. Not so much fear for herself as fear for the rest of us.

"Didn't Salem tell you about the bodies?"

Bodies!

Not the word I wanted to hear this morning.

I twisted around and put my left hand on the porch to hold me up while I brought my gaze around to Salem. She looked less than happy, either because of my penetrating look or because of the nature of the information she was holding. I was betting on information being withheld.

I held my gaze on her until I got any answer.

"Those two are buried about fifty yards out back." Salem made a firm nod toward the picture. "Recently and not deep enough to keep the forest dwellers away."

I was liking our retired detective Green-Jeans less and less as a person. And since I had seen him talking with Loki, it didn't help the pagan's status all that much. I still couldn't image the same level of slime on the big guy.

Loki seemed almost likable.

"Did you find them by smell?"

"Partially. Given another day, we all would have smelled them"—ah, the wonderful benefits of a hot summer day—"but finding a new car track through the brush helped."

It didn't really surprise me that Green-Jeans had been too lazy to carry the bodies out back, but it did that Salem was so willing to share the info with my daughters. It wasn't exactly the best information encouraging them to stay.

"We're going home."

"Good idea, I want my girls safe."

Jody took in a deep breath, a breath that did not bode well for me or my plans.

"We are all going home."

There was a slight hesitation as Jody drew in the second chunk of air.

"Including you and Taylor, even if we have to tie you up."

CHAPTER FIFTY

"What about Salem?"

"Salem is feeding your fantasy."

"My fantasy?"

"We have always known your story wasn't true."

"Always known?"

Jody's voice had softened toward pity, and while she tried hard to continue meeting my eyes, Jody failed, which meant Jess had to inject their sense of truth. "Trees do not grow into children-eating monsters, no matter how old you think they are."

"They don't?"

"We love you, Dad, but you can't really believe a modern store ax can suddenly age into a magical one that sends your enemies away with a puff."

"I can't?"

Jess began following Jody's failure to meet my fast-hardening glare. It was only by each drawing closer together to stand side by side that allowed them to go on. Even then, it took a long pause and interlocking of hands for support to get the next and hardest piece out.

"Think about it, Dad, you were almost sixty and years past running up a steep hill, let alone a mountainside."

"I would have for you."

I am not sure whose eyes held the most pain: Jody's, Jess's, or mine.

Finally, with tears flowing down their cheeks, one of them whispered, "No, you couldn't, Junior could have."

That name hit me like a forty-forty at close range.

I found anything resembling a breath impossible to take in. I think I might have given in right then and there, but I suddenly felt a familiar sense of calm ebb into me, the same one from long ago when Junior and I would eat a breakfast or lunch at the local diner.

We would each be reading our books of choice and only sharing words when a thought needed saying. It was in those quiet moments I think my son and I might have been the closest.

"So I lied?"

"Not really"—Jess looked to Jody for the words before adding their long-hidden belief—"you needed a connection to Junior to go on."

"Can't you understand? We had to let you keep it."

Forty-forty slug number 2 and 3, but this time, I had help resisting their impacts, because I knew the truth. There are things you know in your heart that can never really be explained to those who have not felt them.

"What about me?"

I felt my granddaughter's arm glide around my waist as she moved closer to my side.

"Have I been lying too?"

My twins did a mutual shrug with Jody vocalizing their thought, "Hear a story enough times as a very small child and the tale becomes fact."

So there we were, a duo sitting on a porch edge, while our counterparts did their best to stare us down, each set knowing a different reality, with me and Taylor wanting to follow Robert Frost's path less taken.

"And what about me?"

Salem came off the porch to add a triangle point to our confrontation.

"Am I a fantasy too?"

"You are a nice-enough girl caught up in something too dark and dangerous for our dad."

Salem tilted her head like a cat studying a ball rolling across the floor or a mouse about to pay the price.

My twins broke their handhold to face off against the spread of foes, with Jody drawing the short straw.

"Do you honestly want us to believe you can change into a cat?"

"I do." I placed my hand on Taylor's knee to prevent her speaking first. "I've seen the results."

"Really?" Jess's voice became coated with the tone used with young children or old folk confused by the use of a new phone. "Can you say you have actually seen Salem change into a cat?"

I opened my mouth to answer and let it hang there. I knew in my heart that Salem changed, but I had never actually witnessed the process.

My jaw eased back into place as I considered a new possibility.

Could I be losing it?

Had it all been just a dream like Junior's onetime belief in the reality of the Elf Quest world?

I didn't know but, "Some beliefs take faith."

Not sure if those were my words or a cue coming from another place. Either way, they brought out the last action I had expected.

"I have never showed this to an adult before."

The tenor in Salem's words trapped everyone's attention, except maybe Taylor's. She seemed to shift at my side as if looking away.

But the rest of us saw Salem's borrowed jeans slip off her hips and glide to the ground with nothing under them but skin, followed almost at once by a shirt and bra.

Then, with a grinding compacting of size and skin, a large-sized fur ball of twenty-five-or-so pounds of cat came into being.

CHAPTER FIFTY-ONE

After Salem's changeover production, the twins had little more to say about my leaving. With my role decided, at least in my mind, I took a walk to give Jody and Jess a chance to decide their own path. Taylor and Salem, who, for reasons of her own, had remained in cat form, fell in step before I got in my first half-dozen strides.

I didn't complain.

First of all, I had no idea how to argue such a point with a cat, and second, I wanted Taylor to join me, because, like it or not, if either or both of the twins left, Taylor was going with them.

We went about half a mile toward the main highway before turning back. We were on the last part of our return when I heard the car coming from behind us.

I don't know why I came to a halt. It would only have taken us another twenty steps to reach our turn into the cabin's driveway and out of sight. Probably it was either an old-fashioned sense of nosiness or the hint of a whisper in my mind.

For either of the two reasons, I did a half pivot to look back for the car, standing there until the familiar car came around the curve and stopped dead at the sight of us.

Apparently, retired detective Green-Jeans, who was in the driver's seat, was as surprised as me.

Worse for me, the retired detective wasn't alone.

Green-Jeans had a car full of passengers. From what I could see of them through the windshield, they were Arabs and perhaps the most shocked of all.

To my credit, I was the first to unfreeze.

"Taylor, go warn your aunts!"

To Taylor's credit, she didn't question or argue. She just took off at her best soccer-playing speed to do as I said.

Behind her, Green-Jeans pushed open his door to take up a one-foot-on-the-ground position. Then he put a hand over the door and waved for me to come over to him.

In reply, I just stood there waiting for the retired detective to make his next move, buying time for Taylor to reach her aunts. It wasn't a lot of time, but I figured every moment counted.

Green-Jeans probably thought the same as he slipped the rest of the way out of his car to take up a two-footed position behind its door. Then to further enforce his command, he brought his right hand up over the window, holding an old service revolver.

In answer?

I allowed myself a single glimpse downward to assure myself Salem was on the same page. Then after waving the appropriate finger in the general direction of Green-Jeans, I broke into an awkward gallop of my own, following Salem's stretched-out leaps back toward the cabin.

Even at my old age, I was still fast enough to round into the driveway before Green-Jeans could get off a shot. But from the rev of the motor behind me, I had my doubts about making the porch.

Then the rev of the motor was followed by the screech of the brakes and the sound of a car door being thrown open. It didn't take a genius to know my only hope for staying alive was lousy marksmanship, which was quickly turned off as a factor with the number of rounds the shooter sent in my direction.

What did help was a rough tackle from my right driving the air out of me. But I didn't mind, because as I slammed into the ground, I heard the whine of live rounds passing over me.

It was during the shooter's pause to adjust his sight line to my new position that I heard yet another report.

Only this one came from the cabin.

And after a moment's pause, a second one rang out, leading to the sound of breaking glass.

With the added noise of a car jammed into reverse, I made an effort to get back to my feet, but before I could get my arms square up for the push upward, a giant set of paws hoisted me off the ground instead.

From this new angle, I got a full glance back at the end of the drive, before I found myself being spun to face my Ranger.

Then with more aid than I actually needed, I found myself pushed forward the last few remaining steps before being lifted up and over the tailgate.

As I lay there gathering my wits, I realized three things: The gray hump at the end of the driveway was dead. The hump was not Green-Jeans. And the most important of the three? The person sharing the bed of the Ranger with me was holding my Savage .270 in her hands.

CHAPTER FIFTY-TWO

Being dumped into the bed of my truck, I went flat. With most of my air left behind me, I had little chance to get back even as far as all fours.

In fact, before I could do much of anything, my Ranger jumped forward. A moment later, I was surprised when our driver reached the refuge without slowing down. Even more so when she took the turn lifting at least one tire off the ground.

I would not have considered it bad driving for either of my twins. But from past experience, I was betting at Jody being behind the wheel. Dating back to their very first days of driver's training, she had been the one to show a bit of race car in her blood.

But then I had to wonder who was driving Jody's ride. She wasn't one to let other people drive her ride, and from the dust spewing at us, I figured there was a vehicle in front of us.

And even before I thought my secondary answer, I discarded it.

There was no way my savior was the driver. Squeezing his body into my Ranger would have been a problem for a guy his size, let alone giving him room for the fancy driving my Ranger was doing.

A different time and place, I would have gotten up on my knees to look in through the back window. But now that was out of the question for a couple of reasons.

First of all, a Ranger going down a back road slowly did a lot of bouncing around. At our present speed, it went beyond a hard bouncing, lifting us completely off the floorboard at times.

"Grandpa?"

And there was the second of my reasons.

Taylor's hands were so tightly wrapped around my .270 Savage she had nothing left to soften her bounces. This shaking around might have been the cause for Taylor's paleness, but knowing my granddaughter, I suspected something more.

"Taylor?"

"Grandpa"—Taylor's face downshifted into an even paler shade of white—"did I kill him?"

Truth now? Or truth later?

Either way, it wasn't going to make it easier on my granddaughter with the soft heart. I had known Taylor to shed a tear at the sight of a dead fawn on the side of the road.

"Did I?" The grip on my .270 Savage tightened another degree with the beginning of a tear forming in her eye. "I saw him spin away from you and go down but didn't have time for anything else."

The tear moved forward with the next rut in the road, only to lunge off her nose to land in the bed between us.

Right then I could have lied.

Probably should have, but I didn't.

"He wasn't moving."

"And in the car?"

Green-Jeans's car was already out of my sight line by the time I could check it out. And even if Taylor had hit someone, it would have been hard to tell.

The only thing I could say for sure, it wasn't the driver or the Arabs would have still have been sitting there. And Taylor might still be sending .270 rounds in their direction.

Somehow, I held back the beginning of a wicked grin.

Inside my head, I had to admit the idea of having Green-Jeans bleeding out behind the wheel didn't break my heart. But having Taylor bear the burden of another killing didn't seem like a good idea at the moment.

"Where did you hit the windshield?"

Taylor closed her eyes, as if recalling the moment. "Just off-center to the driver's side at a steep angle."

That info came at me with a conflicted emotion.

Missing the driver at that angle for sure meant a complete miss. Therefore, it didn't lower the odds against us. But even more important in my mind at least, being just a harmless window breaker would not add a further burden on to Taylor's heart.

"Then you probably gave retired detective Green-Jeans some smelly pants, but I can't see how you hit anyone."

My answer brought a hint of color back into Taylor's face but did not to chase away her troubled expression, only seeming to change it from sad to shame.

"Guess I am not as strong as my dad."

I took a dozen bumps recalling how Junior's eyes were matching blue to those I was looking into now. And as for a soft heart, a fluffy cloud would have been harder.

Checking the pain in my granddaughter's eye brought a much-remembered quote from my son to my mind. Those words would address Taylor's pain better than anything I had to say.

"I have been told your dad did a lot of killing in Iraq"—I got a finger pointed at Taylor for accent—"but never once did he claim the shooting was done in self-defense."

Taylor's eyes took on a faraway gleam.

It seemed as if Taylor was hearing the words from her father as much as from me.

"Your dad told me he only killed to protect his buddies." I felt a faraway whisper in my ear telling me to add, "I would say his daughter has that same type of character."

Now the tears in Taylor's eyes really began to flow. And in spite of the bouncing around, she managed to edge closer to me.

"Maybe because we were both raised by the same man."

CHAPTER FIFTY-THREE

Now with both of us being tongue-tied, the taking got easier.

It came about as my Ranger turned off the main road. The bounce in the airspeed leaked off to a stay-in-place roughness rattling your teeth. Besides the bounce's shrinking, the overhanging dust drifted away behind us to be replaced by a ceiling of low-hanging pine branches, a few of them hanging so low they rolled over the cab's roof with a thump and snap as they broke away from the main branches.

But best of all, the slower speed allowed me to reach out and loosen Taylor's grip on my rifle. I didn't try to take the .270 away from my granddaughter, but the relaxation of her grip allowed for a renewed flow of blood into Taylor's fingers.

The loosening also helped with Taylor's facial color.

It went from bleached-out white to teenager flushed.

"I didn't get to warn my aunts." My face must have shown some puzzlement, because she hurried on, "Loki had already reached the cabin and given the alarm."

"Loki?"

"Aunt Jess claimed he just suddenly popped out of the woods." Taylor's hunched-up shoulders told me there was not much more to say about Loki. "When I ran up, Aunt Jess and Jody were clearing our stuff out of the cabin for a quick exit."

"And you grabbed the .270."

"Not really, Loki shoved it into my hands and plunked me into the bed of your Ranger." Taylor gave me a screwed-up, mixed-up "half frown, half smile" expression. "I thought Loki might want some covering fire."

Whether Loki wanted it or not, I was glad Taylor gave it.

But bringing up the dead-body results did not seem the best way to keep my granddaughter calm.

"Where are we going?"

Taylor looked up at the branches overhead, studying the overhead air sweeping before giving up a squeak, "Back to town?"

"I don't think so."

My eyes joined Taylor's staring at the overgrowth. We might have been taking a secret passage to avoid being followed, but from what I could tell, we were going the wrong direction. Upward, toward the mountainside and away from safety.

Twenty minutes later, the Ranger came to a halt.

A moment later, even before Taylor and I got used to the lack of bounce, Salem burst into view on my side of the Ranger bed.

I guessed, from her outfit, Salem had done a quick grab of wardrobe. Little of it was her own.

The T-shirt was the Johnny Cash one I had used yesterday, and the jeans were not Salem's usual fit. They were a tight fit through the hips, which made them most likely a pair of Taylor's.

Mine and even the twins' would have fit more like a pair of clown pants.

Salem's long sliver hair was folded up into a ponytail style. Not an unseen hairdo in itself, but this time, it had a number of strands flying loose, which was a new look.

Jody shadowed Salem with her own look, unchanged since our talk of a while ago, except for one tiny detail: Jody was holding a familiar handgun in her left hand, and it looked ready for use.

"Come on, Dad." I found Jody's right hand reaching down to aid my dismount. "We're going up the mountainside."

I hesitated with my hand hanging halfway to Jody's.

"Say what?"

Jody made a grab for my hanging hand and hauled me up into a sitting position. "We don't have a choice."

We always had a choice.

But for the moment, I just slipped over the side to take a stance next to Jody, which I barely established before I found my forty-four jammed into my hand.

Worse than the jolt of the jamming was the shock of Loki moving up behind Jody. From the size of the rescuer who tossed me into my Ranger, I had half expected him to be here.

Still! I had questions to ask, with the first question doing a quick change of subject, from asking Loki what was going on to why the sounds of gunfire were suddenly coming from down our back trail.

CHAPTER FIFTY-FOUR

"Loki!"

Loki's attention shifted from the sound of gunfire to me without the slightest hint of guile or surprise. I thought he would have at least waited for me to ask my question, but he didn't.

"With the cat-lady guardian back in their sights, the Arabs seemed to be eliminating their competition." Loki's eyes took a knowing survey of the girls. "And common sense told me that eliminating would include your family."

I held my hand palm up toward the firing.

"My dad, he brought in our men this morning." Loki read my mind and kept going. "We thought it best to house them out of sight, believing I was enough of a presence to find your silver-haired friend."

"With retired detective Green-Jeans's help."

Loki's cool did not actually crack, but I could have sworn his jawlines hardened. And just maybe his blue eyes lost a bit of friendliness.

"The retired detective is a perfect example of what is wrong with law enforcement in your country." Loki's voice tightened the tiniest bit with each word. "Not even money can buy his loyalty, let alone a cause."

I thought about it a moment and answered Loki with a comment of my own, "I would have never believed it."

"What?"

Okay, maybe our giant's cool was showing a hairline crack, and Taylor jumping in did more than widen it a bit.

"Grandpa is shocked that anyone could think less of the so-called retired detective than he did."

I could almost hear the next comment coming out of Taylor's mouth. But for the life of me, I could not think of a single reason for stopping it.

"Grandpa would not trust Green-Jeans to wipe our dog's ass."

So much for Loki's cool attitude.

It disappeared with Loki's deep-down belly laugh, and in spite of the tenseness, I joined in with an all-out laugh of my own, and everyone else followed suit, even my girl Jess, who had only united with us in time to hear Taylor's final part of the conversation.

I don't think any of us would have been unhappy if Taylor's second shot had been placed a little differently in Green-Jeans's windshield, Except maybe for Taylor, who didn't need a second death on her heart. At least not at this age.

Still!

I turned back to the questioning.

"The shooting?"

"My dad also believes in eliminating the competition." Loki must have read my mine and added, "But only if they are a threat to our own safety."

I chewed over Loki's admission, wondering if our relationship to Salem might be a prescribed threat as well. At another time and place, I would have asked.

But under the present circumstances, I wasn't sure I trusted or wanted to hear Loki's answer.

I also didn't want to hear what Loki said next, but I didn't have a choice.

Loki wasn't talking to me.

He was talking to Salem.

"Now shall we go after the Witch Rose?"

"To retrieve or destroy?" I stepped between Salem and the big guy before she had a chance to answer on her own.

Loki studied my face, knowing the answer I wanted and refusing to give it to me. Instead, he peeled off in a different direction I wanted to hear even less.

"Legend says we once had a Witch Rose of our own." Loki took a wide step to bring his sight line in to view of Salem. "The Romans destroyed it with fire."

Loki hesitated before adding more, and I found Salem's arm intertwining with my own.

"And its guardian died as well."

CHAPTER FIFTY-FIVE

Salem didn't wait for me to make eye contact.

With a single step, Salem broke arm contact and was past me on her way to the front of my Ranger. Once there, she jerked open the door and grabbed up a six packs of plastic water bottles from in front of the passenger seat.

There, without a real hesitation, Salem broke apart the bundle and tossed each of the bottles toward a pair of waiting hands. Except for Loki, he got a connect pair, having earned the privilege by passing mine on to me.

Still without any eye contact, Salem began moving up toward the front end of our caravan. Leaving the rest of us behind, she began gathering up needed supplies. And once the twins' backpacks were emptied of clothes and filled with such items as extra water and guns, we were on the go.

Salem stopped at a point just off the lead vehicle's right-hand door and waited for us. I should have hustled to be first in line, but I hung back to wonder how Jess's ride had joined us.

It should have been parked back in town at the inn, but now it was here just in front of my Ranger. But the question was answered by another Norse man stationed just to the far side of it.

"Loki promised he would stay here to watch our back," Jody answered my question as she edged past.

I glanced over at Jody with an unspoken "Sure" on my lips.

I should have halted Jody right then and there, but while I hated to admit it, the time for questioning had passed with Salem stepping away. The best I could do was follow her lead and hope for the best, which led us into the heavy brush leading first across and then up the early part of the mountainside. It was not an easy pathway, and Salem set a hard pace. I would have fallen behind and gotten lost within the first ten minutes, but for three guardians—Loki and my twins—they seemed to have worked out an unspoken method of dropping back in rotation to help me along, with only Taylor and Salem not joining in to offer a helping hand or shoulder to keep me going.

By the time we stepped out into the brushless area of the cabins, my fatigue left me with just enough energy to drain the last of my water bottle and suck in air like a landlocked fish gulping for air.

I wavered at the edge with a twin to either side, as they took in the location of my folktale for the very first time.

Three cabins and a host of nightmares they should never have joined.

The first of the buildings had changed a little over the years, but not like the others. The second seemed to have aged five years for each of ours. And the third was little more than a minimal skeleton of boards. And as we got closer, the scene worsened beyond the aging of the woodwork.

The building had an unnatural rot gushing out toward us.

It was only an unpleasantness in the remembered first cabin from my long-ago visit. It was a different smell but had the same sense of stink that you got from a roadside flash of freshly flattened black and white.

The odor coming at us from the second of the two buildings was worse, like a mixture of sewer rot and swamp gas. It hammered my guts with the pounding of a butter churn, and from the looks of my girls, they weren't faring much better.

Even the big fella's face claimed a less-than-normal coloring.

And with the third?

I sensed more than smelled the stench.

There was the clinging of ancient rot hanging over the remaining structure like a halo of brimstone. I think going closer might have overpowered my sense of smell and humanity to drive me beyond crazy.

"It's the remains of long-dead children clinging to hold on the to last remnants of the Witch Rose."

Salem was talking to my twins, but her eyes were on mine— yeah, meeting mine for the first time since releasing my arm by the Ranger, as if daring me to choose between keeping her in my life and going through with the destruction of such an evil.

Not a fair place to leave me.

CHAPTER FIFTY-SIX

I had been breathing hard and stumbling all too often over the last hundred yards.

Still, I would have rather kept going up toward the Witch Rose. Whether I liked the final results to come or not, I needed this thing to be over.

But Loki thought different about us moving on from the cabins. To slow down our departure, he pointed out the signs of my fatigue to the girls. And this time, even Taylor, my loyal granddaughter, was against me pushing on.

Salem was the only one not saying anything against me moving on. She almost seemed to support me with her eyes.

But then again.

After giving our big guy another study, she suggested we move inside, saying the best of the three cabins would give us a place to sit and recover.

I don't know why I gave in. But in the end, anything to get me closer to the mountainside seemed a move in the right direction, even if only a few steps.

Once in the cabin, I would let my mouth carry us on from there.

Loki stepped forward to gather up the twins' backpacks. Then he waved the girls over to help me toward the closest of the cabins that was still standing. We set off as a foursome, with Salem hesitating an extra minute to grab some more water out of Jody's pack.

Once we were inside the cabin, the odor dropped off to a background smell coming from outside. I found it wasn't all that hard to handle and the water offered around by Salem helped.

I was halfway into my first gulp when I noticed Loki had not followed after us. He was still at the edge of the clearing, but now he was no longer alone.

The guy we had left behind with our rides was with him.

Apparently, promises given to non-Norsemen were not meant to be kept.

"Did you expect anything else?"

"No, but everyone else was hoping?"

"Not me or Salem." I glanced over at Salem disappearing into the next room as Taylor added, "Remember, we got a glimpse of his father."

I could see that.

So why did we bring him along?

Because he got us this far intact with our guns.

Or did he?

Loki had my .270 Savage slung over his shoulder and the backpacks at his feet. Dressed for the heat, I could tell neither of my twins were packing their handguns.

So as far as I could tell, the only gun left in our hands was my forty-four revolver, or so I thought.

A check of my back pockets and belt proved otherwise.

"Anybody take my forty-four from me coming up here?"

Jody shook her head, but Jess took a half moment to think about the question.

And then?

"Loki took it while you were stumbling over the worst of the rough stuff"—Jess looked to see where Loki was as her words trailed off—"I'm sure he was holding on to your gun for safekeeping and is going to return it."

Jody followed Jess's gaze and had the truth click to the front of her thinking. Her gaze came back to me as she mouthed, "And we are now unarmed and trapped."

I nodded, but the voice from behind said otherwise.

"Not trapped."

The twins looked past me at the voice, and I assumed Taylor's shuffle off to my side was her doing the same. Me, I just continued staring out the door, hoping yet dreading what I was going to hear.

"But you won't like the exit." Salem made no move to get closer to us. "The only thing I can promise you is, it will get us out of this place and up the mountainside out of sight."

"Without any weapons."

I did a super slow pivot to face my silver-haired lady in time to see the end of her shrug. I didn't see that being the answer any of the girls wanted to see.

But at the same time, I didn't think they would like mine any better.

CHAPTER FIFTY-SEVEN

Salem led us into what passed for a kitchen and pointed to a familiar structure in the middle of the room.

It was a lot like an old-time dumbwaiter, the one used in a lot of multilevel homes to bring meals up from the kitchen and then afterward take the dishes and remains back down.

And I didn't like this one.

Salem had once tried to get Taylor to drop down this hole. We stopped Salem, only to have her take Taylor out the front window and up the mountainside a few minutes later.

That was then; this is now.

"On the back wall, you will find a small ridge. Behind it, the ground will slope down, out and under the back wall"—Salem made air motions with her hands to accent the directions—"go straight out the fifteen yards and you will find a padded door to push through."

"How heavy?"

Salem looked at me with a depth of sadness I didn't want to see. It was too much like a memory from the time of Father's rule, when the Father and his followers terrorized my granddaughter and countless other children.

"It was made to keep the leftover spirits of children in." Salem's eyes wandered toward Taylor. "None of us should have any trouble pushing it open."

Taylor and Salem exchanged a look, a nod, and Taylor's completion of the thought: "Easy enough for a five-year-old to push open back then."

There was a little unspoken murmuring between the twins and another hard-look exchange between Salem and Taylor. I had to wonder if any of them were thinking of my problem with small spaces.

"I'll go first."

I almost looked around at their faces to see who was volunteering. But since the voice was masculine, it eliminated everybody but me.

And I found all the eyes around me confirming the fact.

I waved away any of their protests before they started and stepped over to a cupboard. I wish the opening had grown a little bigger, or even a lot bigger. But I had to admit, it was down beneath, which scared me the most.

After all, we wouldn't be able to see anything down there.

What if the walls were too close together or, even worse, in bad condition and ready to fall in on me? And even if the room below was in good shape, what about the slope leading away? What if it was too tight for my shoulders?

I was wider than any of the girls.

I could get trapped between the two walls.

Then what?

Could the girls push me through or at least pull me out so they could go on without me?

Or what if, during those efforts, the walls caved in on us?

It might leave the girls trapped forever, and I certainly didn't want to die like that, alone and unable to breathe anything but dirt. Anything but that.

Still.

"Dark and tight?"

"The room below us is plenty big." Salem moved shoulder to shoulder with me. "The tunnel going away could be bigger, but I wouldn't suggest it if I thought any of us would get stuck."

"I don't like tight spots."

"Want me to go first?"

I shook off Salem's offer, thinking I really didn't want any of us to go down there. I wanted to take my girls and to march out the front door and up the mountainside to the Witch Rose's clearing.

I reached out to open the lift so I could squeeze in and get started. But a touch on my arm slowed me down.

"Ignore the squish." Salem's eyes did a duck and dodge to avoid mine. "Just walk straight to the exit."

"Squish?"

Salem's nod was more toward the front of the cabin than toward any of us.

"Mud? Garbage?"

Salem eyes came back to me and locked in like a mouse with a snake, afraid to stay still, even more afraid to move.

"Remains…"

"Of the children you fed to the Witch Rose."

Salem nodded to me, to the twins, and finally to Taylor. I don't have any idea of what their eyes said to each other. But to the granddaughter's credit, Taylor's eyes held the least doubt of any of us.

"Once the Witch Rose got a taste of the child, it lived off each cell's energy long after the child had died."

"But the other cabins…"

"Have been modernized and rebuilt over and over since the time where the first one was a mere hole in the ground." Salem never checked the girls for belief; her words were meant for me alone. "There were only two cabins here when I became the replacement guardian."

There were so many more questions to ask.

But they would have to wait.

CHAPTER FIFTY-EIGHT

Squeezing into the dumbwaiter took more than a bit of effort with some added crimping by Jody as well. And then came the lowering into the dark.

Crammed into the dumbwaiter, I felt like a shucked-off sock, all out of shape and dropping in the blindness of the clothes hamper under the other clothes.

As the light faded away and disappeared into darkness, I wanted to scream out in panic. But I couldn't; I had to hold on for my kids.

Touching down was both a relief and a terror.

I was able to unglue my tongue from the roof of my mouth and suck in a breath. It wasn't the best of air, heavy with the taste of mold. But suffering from the worst of tastes was still a lot better than passing out from lack of air.

The other side of the issue was the terror of moving forward into the dark. It would get me out of the confinement of the dumbwaiter, but I couldn't see my own eyelids. What if stepping out would sink me into the ooze trapping me in place or, worse, flowing over my head?

I didn't want to smother that way—or any other way, for that matter.

I crunched the first leg out of the waiter and down toward the ground.

The ground was not as bad as I thought.

It was mushy but more like moss than mud, and I got my second leg down into it without being sucked under. Even the full placement of my body weight went on to the ooze without any real sinkage.

I orientated myself by reaching back to the dumbwaiter. It was already going back up, but I got just a graze of the bottom and used that to move through the darkness toward the back wall.

And after several gushy strides, I found the ridge mentioned by Salem and the emptiness behind it, which brought about another problem.

The slope on the other side of the ridge went down.

What if I went over the ten-inch ridge and slid down into a cave-in?

From what I could tell, the tunnel going down was only a little wider than my shoulder, with maybe six-inch leverage on either side.

Once into it, I didn't think there would be enough room to get turned around or get the leverage to push myself back up against the angle. And if the cave-in was far enough down the slope, my girls would be helpless.

"Dad?"

I had missed the creak of the dumbwaiter's return and almost waited a second time for Jody's callout. But it was as if I sensed her next inhale and forced myself to direct her to my side.

Once there, she fumbled into a hand-holding.

"What me to go first, Dad?"

Of course.

I didn't want to go at all.

The only thing worse might be staying here in the black.

"No!" I drew in a deep breath and let out a long exhale. "Just make sure you pull me out or push me through if I get stuck."

I should have waited for Jess and the others to join us, but it was quickly becoming a now-or-never moment.

And nothing left my girls dangling between my fears and Loki's people.

Without taking time for another word, I edged up over the ridge and started my slide down the other side. By keeping both hands out front, I was able to maintain a hold on my speed. Not that it helped with the narrowing of the tunnel.

Every time I bumped a side or raised my head up toward the ceiling, I knew the sides were moving in on me. A little more and

I would be trapped, unable to move forward or back, and the air seemed to get harder to suck in.

I kept telling myself it was all in my head, but my head told me I was lying.

I didn't think I could handle another drop forward, even so much as a foot or even four inches. When on top of everything else, my escape closed off.

There was no more empty air for my fingers to reach through, just a solid wall. And my shoulders told me there was no bend going off in either direction.

Worst of all, there was no way I could force myself back up, and the kids were too far away to help.

If my daughters tried, they would only slide down into me and make the plug thicker and harder to get out of. In spite of everything, all my efforts to maintain my self-control, I broke.

The churn started down in my guts and began a race toward freedom.

Then I choked it off.

CHAPTER FIFTY-NINE

About three inches above the slope line going down, the dirt turned into a matting of sorts. Not sure what the material was but praying for the best, I lifted my other hand up to join the first.

And then I pushed.

The whole thing swung out as a large square and dropped away to the side. Then I found myself searching for sight as the tree-shadowed daylight flashed away the darkness.

"Grandpa?"

"We're out." I let myself slide down to the lip and propped the head off to one side. "Just give me a moment to get myself over the lip and out, then you can start coming down and join me."

It took more than a moment to wiggle myself over the lip, but the girls waited until I gave them the go-ahead. And when Taylor followed down in my slide path, I was able to catch her under the arms and help lift her over the lip.

With the two of us at the bottom, Jody and Jess were more trusting. They came down feetfirst and needed a lot less help, while Salem, being more catlike, needed no help at all.

The real problem began once we were on our feet with different destinations in mind.

Jody and Jess wanted to go toward the highway and retreat out of our situation. While in direct contrast to their wishes, Salem and I wanted to continue up the mountainside, with Taylor leaning toward her grandpa's side but hesitant with the thought of possibly having to kill another person.

"We have to get help." Jess started to make steps toward the downward trail, while Jody tried to gather in Taylor's hand.

"From who?"

"The authorities."

"You do that." I turned my eyes away from Taylor, hoping the twins would take her along for her own safety. "I am going up the mountainside with Salem."

"Unarmed?"

"For now." Jody saw my "but" even before I added, "Your brother will provide."

I got skyward eye rolls from my twins in chorus. And Taylor's own look was less than encouraging.

"Junior is dead." Jody stayed in the lead, but Jess was in nodding agreement. "And I don't want to go rock throwing against bullets."

"Then don't."

I turned away from my girls and began moving toward Salem, who was on the side of our group nearest the climb upward. I figured she would swivel around to lead me toward the remaining bits of the Witch Rose.

Salem didn't.

When I reached the spot even with her, Salem's hand came out to grasp my arm. It didn't have enough hold to stop my march, but I came to a halt anyway.

"Taylor?" Salem's eyes never came around to mine. She just continued to stare at the girls.

It was the rustle of movement coming up beside Salem that told me of Taylor's choice. After that, an in-chorus growl from behind told me the rest.

"Damn you, Dad."

CHAPTER SIXTY

To get to our takeoff point going up the mountainside, we had to go past number 2 and 3 cabins. With each pace toward the second cabin, the stench grew, until it reached its height directly behind the cabin.

I have probably smelled worse, but at that moment, I could not remember when. It really outdid any diaper change within memory, and over the years, my kids had managed some of the worst.

I didn't have much in my stomach, and for once, I was glad I had gone without breakfast. As it was, my gut went to war with my stomach, doing everything possible to empty out some phlegm. But I kept it locked up behind clenched teeth and a locked jaw.

Not everybody was so lucky.

At least one of my ladies following behind let everything go. And a chorus of gagging told me the others were going to follow her example sooner or later.

At least the back of the cabin was a small distance to cover and the walking was gentle enough to allow a quickstep pace. And I figured after that, it couldn't get any worse.

A few steps past the number 2 cabin forced me to reevaluate that thought. If anything, passing cabin 2 had been a picnic.

Two paces into crossing cabin 3's downwind side, my stomach sent the phlegm right past my teeth and jaws before I had a chance to steal them.

It forced me over at the waist and grasping for something more to bring up. I found my knees wobbling and the urge to go down almost unstoppable.

Behind me, the twins and Taylor were following suit, with Jess already down on one knee and Taylor wavering between one knee and total collapse.

Even Salem had lost her color and was having a real struggle trying to pull Jess back to her feet. It took power I had never ever had to force myself two steps back to haul Jody up straight and even more to push her toward the far side of the cabin.

As I got Jody to the far edge and stumbling toward what had to be better air, I turned first to Jess and then Taylor.

Salem had Jess back up to her feet, but they were having trouble getting that first step in line. Taylor was still in a bent-over situation, with both hands on her knees to hold her up, but inching herself along in a shuffle.

Both needed help, but I would be lucky to aid either.

Sucking it up hard, I took a step toward the closer girl and forced Taylor up straight. Then like a drunken team in a three-legged race, we weaved our way after Jody.

Thinking back, I am not sure who helped the other the most. I would like to say, since I am the elder, it was me helping Taylor. But at the same time, I have to admit, Taylor kept more than one of my stumbles from being a fall.

The stink didn't halt at the end of cabin, but it eased down with every pace. Twenty yards past the cabin and out of the downwind, I was ready to push Taylor on and turn back to help Jess.

But I didn't get a chance.

I found Jody's hand grabbing my shoulder to pull us forward. And then as I passed her, she whispered hoarsely into my ear, "Keep going. I'll give Jess and Salem a hand. They are right behind you."

A good father would have been the one to go back and help. But the best I had ever claimed was one who tried hard.

Jody stepped past me into the stink to gather up the other set of strugglers. Within moments, we were in the "it stinks, but I have smelled worse" area. And with a few more strides, everyone's gagging was under control.

We probably could have all used a rest period, but none of us wanted to wait around for Loki's father to check out cabin number 1.

It was bad enough we had to cross the out-of-sight corner of the clearing. It would have only taken Loki or his father one curious moment to put our corner into their sight line.

I forced myself to start forward, hoping the others would fall in line, only glimpsing back a few steps later to find Jody standing next to a stump reaching down.

As I watched, Jody came up with a pair of poles used for gardening tool handles. From my position, I could see where the metal ends had been twisted to screw into a hoe or shovel.

Too bad they didn't have one of those screwed in. But as Jody handed one pair to Jess, I couldn't help thinking they were better than nothing.

The twinge following that thought reminded me of a similar gift from Junior on this same mountainside. It had also been left by a tree stump for me to find.

CHAPTER SIXTY-ONE

J ust my luck.

The climb had gotten three times as steep since my first climb.

Chasing after Salem and Taylor, I had gone up the same mountainside at a run, as I remember, not even losing my breath once.

But now?

I went into a stumble every tenth step. And while I could blame part of that on our passage behind the cabin, all the girls seemed to have shaken off the experience.

After a short distance, Taylor had moved up to my side. Once there, she jammed a hand into my armpit to aid my balance. I should have waved her off but didn't have the breath or pride to do so.

That really helped for a while, but I outweighed my granddaughter by more than half her weight again. Before long, Taylor and I were having difficulties as a couple. Twice we almost went down on all fours.

And the twins noticed on the second time.

As I got to my feet, I suddenly found my arm pulled away and dragged over Jody's shoulder. Meanwhile, on the other side of my body, Taylor's arm was edged out, and Jess took up the same position as her sister.

I hated to admit it, but the next part of the climb became easier. The slope was no less steep, but with the twins' support, I got back ten years of stamina.

Even then, we had to take a couple of breaks for all-around deep breaths, mostly because of my extra weight on the twins, but passed it off as Taylor's tender age.

Right! Like my granddaughter could not outwalk us all on a bad day and still have enough energy left over to host a sleepover with her teammates.

It was at the second of these stops that I noticed the tip of Jody's garden handle. It was no longer sporting a metal screw in for attachment. The tip had lengthened out several inches and had developed ancient markings trailing up a third of the handle's length.

I gave Jody a shoulder bump to get her attention. Once we had eye contact, I directed Jody's eyes toward the garden handle she had been using as a walking stick.

Jody's eye did a slow widen, and she grunted Jess's attention toward the same tip. After a momentary checking out of her own, Jess brought what had been a matching garden handle up for inspection.

Unlike Jody's handle, Jess's tip was triple pronged. But unlike a pitchfork you used for garden work, the prongs seemed more war-like. And a length of the wood had the same ancient symbols running away from the tip toward Jess's handhold.

"Still think I was lying about Junior?"

"He is dead, Dad."

"I know." I rubbed my fingertip over the blunted edge of Jess's trident, and while I know it is impossible, the ends seemed to be getting sharper. "But perhaps not gone."

A visible shiver went through each of the twins as they exchanged a look with each other and then the changing tips. I am not sure what they were thinking, but they reached out their hands to me.

Only this time, I felt a lot younger and waved them off. Then before they could stop me, I began my own climb up the mountainside.

Not sure how the twins liked the idea, but all the same, they fell back a couple of steps without any verbal objections.

Still, it was a good thing our next climb took us into the clearing of the Witch Rose, because while I had yet to feel a drain on the new energy burst, I was not sure how long the spurt would last.

Looking around the clearing, I'm not sure if I was glad or sad about the burst lasting this long.

This clearing bought back a lot of bad memories.

The grass was still dead around the edges of the clearing, and the boulder supporting the Witch Rose was also in place. Except this time, the Witch Rose was not draped over the rock. The only real remaining sign of its onetime presence was a blackened scar running across the lower third of the stone.

Walking closer, I took in the crack leading down under the boulder. It seemed large enough from across the clearing, but standing here, I could see where it would take a downward slide of several feet to reach the last of the Witch Rose, with the gap narrowing all the way.

Not a trip I wanted any of us to take.

CHAPTER SIXTY-TWO

"The size of that crack will make your little girl very useful."

I spun to face the voice coming from the edge of the clearing, a different point from where we had just entered the clearing, and there was more than just one speaker.

There were five pagans standing there, but only one was important. That was the old man, one step in front and the only one talking.

The other four were large men, but none of them matched up in size to Loki or his father. At the moment, they were flanked out in a V behind the old pagan but still close enough to shield their leader from us with a single step.

All of them were double armed, carrying both a modern rifle and pistol along with a collection of axes and clubs. And from the way they were carried, I was guessing these men knew how to use all of them.

"And the rest of us?"

"You I need." The old man at the waist to face Salem. "The others have no value to me."

Salem may have been the one asking the question, but the old man's answer disturbed us all. I personally didn't like the idea of someone saying my twins had no value.

After all, they meant the world to me.

The situation was upgraded to worse with the old's man next command. He turned to the man on his left and ordered him to call in the rest of his people.

Taking on five of the old man's pagans was far from ideal. Adding more men to his side didn't help our odds.

Funny part of the guy's attempt was the fact that cell phones had never worked up here. A sane man would have called it a dead spot. But according to Salem, nothing requiring technology from the last two thousand years worked around the Witch Rose, especially the most modern stuff from the last trio of decades.

It was almost funny to watch the old man's peon fiddling around trying to get reception. From what I could tell, he got nothing on the phone, not even static. After several unsuccessful attempts, he held the cell palm up to the old man with a "Now what?" look on his face.

The old man gave his guy a snort before reaching over to the ram's horn at his side. Without even giving the guy a second chance, he proved the horn was for more than decoration.

With his head tilted back, he raised up the horn to his lips and blew.

The resulting blast seemed to echo back at us from all directions. And it seemed like even before the first echo had rebounded a second time, our recent friend Loki stepped into view from yet another part of the clearing with two companions of his own.

He took a single long look around the clearing at all of us and sighed. "You should have stayed at the cabin and trusted me."

"Better that they didn't." The old man took a crabbing side step toward his son. "We will need the girl to reach the Witch Rose."

"The hell you do"—I waved Taylor toward the twins—"none of us are going to help you."

The old pagan gave me a dismissing look and motioned at the guy to his side. "Kill him!"

Both Loki and Jody moved to stop the old man's command, but neither had an angle. The guy's rifle was up, with the trigger pulled before they could reach the shooter.

But like the cell phone, the rifle went click with no report. And before he could get off a second trigger pull to see if the first attempt was a misfire, Jody rammed her lance into the middle of the shooter's sternum.

And then, shocking to everyone but Salem and me, the guy didn't cry out or bleed.

He simply twinkled away into the air and was gone.

CHAPTER SIXTY-THREE

Even though I was not shocked by the twinkling away, I was out-reacted by two others.

First, since the rifle had been dropped before the twinkling, it had to follow its owner. Before anyone else thought to move, another of the old man's group, the closest of his followers, went down on one knee to grab for the fallen rifle.

Still, even with his quickness, the move for the fallen weapon wasn't swift enough.

The pagan got his hands on the rifle all right. But as his fingers touched the stock; Jess's trident trapped his hand against the ground. The main points of the tridents all missed hitting flesh, but the sharpened inside hooks did. They sliced through the man's wrist like a piece of soft cheese.

But again, no blood, just a twinkling away to nothing.

Only worse for us, Jess was not the last to react.

With surprising speed, the old giant took a single stride toward Jess. Then with a roar, he brought his ram's horn down on Jess's trident.

Thanks to Jess's own quickness, the blow was only a glancing one. But that was enough.

The tri-bladed head dangled from a point four inches above the end of the handle. In reality, the killing part was still attached, but not with the firmness to do any stabbing.

And to further stack the odds, the old man's pagans were joining him by twos and threes. Already their total had reached the far side of a score with what seemed like more to come.

Not exactly the way I wanted to play our confrontation out.

Even with help from beyond, we could only handle so much.

And much was getting mucher by the moment.

Now I knew it was my job to even up the odds in our favor or at least buy some time for Jess's trident to heal.

Because in our favor, the end of Jess's weapon was pulling itself back together fiber by wooden fiber. At the moment, the trident was nowhere close to being healed back into a weapon of supernatural destruction. The angle of dangling had gone from a waving ninety degrees to a stiffening sixty degrees.

"Hey, old man!"

It might have been my words but more likely the volume that got everyone's attention. After all, I had been a coach once and did know how to empty my lungs in a loud manner, including my target.

Loki's father gave me the look of a lion studying a pesty field mouse. Since he was now here in front of the Witch Rose, I wasn't even worth the effort to get angry.

"What are you going to do when I destroy the last of the Witch Rose?"

"You can't!"

The old man began turning his attention to my armed daughters when I rattled it back to me.

"Want to bet?"

This time, the eyes coming around were slitted, and I was worth the effort to get upset. "You won't fit!"

"I'll suck in my gut."

"And are you willing to destroy Salem as well?"

With his father in charge, I hadn't expected Loki to join in.

And to tell the truth, I wish Loki had stayed out of it, because I didn't really like the point he was making.

I tried to weigh all the points of future children against the possible present loss of Salem. But with everything else going on, I couldn't wrap my mind around either loss.

Finally, I gave up thinking of a solution and looked to Salem.

Salem didn't smile, frown, or show any emotions.

She just gave me a nod and watched from the far end of the crease as I dived into the crack.

CHAPTER SIXTY-FOUR

I led with my hands and used them to slow me down, the idea being to not get stuck. But they didn't work well enough to prevent a star spinning head bump on the way down or halt my sliding crunch between ceiling and slope inches short of the bottom.

I fought through the spinning spots with enough sense of mind to reach down with my right hand. Swinging it back and forth between the narrowing gap, I scraped the top of something rough but living.

I tried reaching out to get a grip on it but fell short. I missed having the length to get a hold on it by two inches or a little less. Finally, in desperation, I blew all the remaining air out of my lungs and slipped down another two and a half inches.

The inches gave me the reach I needed to get a hold on the rough leaf, first with my right hand and then both. I still had to finger walk my grip down an inch further before I got the grip I wanted.

Even then, the stub of the Witch Rose did not want to come out of the ground. I gave the plant my hardest tug and got nothing. I tried working it back and forth, but while it gave a bit, it didn't pop loose.

I tried pulling straight out again, and this time I gained a full inch. Then, with the Witch Rose a bit looser, I gave it a couple of hard jerks in either direction. And suddenly, it came loose in my hands, and I was able to work my fingers down into its main body.

It was a tennis-sized gob of goo that throbbed against my fingertips. I don't know why, but something told me the goo is what I had to destroy.

I flipped it up with my fingers to get a two-handed hold on the pulsing bulb and let loose an airless scream.

I couldn't stand it.

The goo burned with a pain beyond imagination. It wasn't a burn of heat or extremely cold. This burn came from a million years of hate and evil and was driving everything else right out of my mind.

There was no smell, sight, or touch left in my world, just red.

Somewhere else I knew I was supposed to do something, but no matter how I tried, I could not remember what it was.

Then there was a dim break at the corner or the red.

It was hazy and out of focus, but I knew what it was.

It was a well-known blond, shifting from five years of age through the seasons until she became a teenager. A beautiful youngster with many a remembered smile and tears.

Even as it appeared, the spot was crowded to the one side by a pair of twins playing in the pool with their younger brother then with separate walks down the aisle.

The visions were then followed by a grave site in Arlington and the feel of two hands closing around mine.

And with the power of my family behind me, I squeezed both hands together and felt the ooze of goo spreading out between my fingers. It was then the pictures, the red, and everything else faded toward black.

I tried to hold on to something, but I couldn't.

And black got darker as every feeling disappeared except a familiar voice calling me forward.

But while the voice was Junior's voice, it was saying the wrong words.

It sounded more like "go back" than a welcome.

CHAPTER SIXTY-FIVE

I never came out of the darkness, at least not on the mountainside, or on the ride to the hospital.

I had some vague sensations of being bounced and shots of pain. But nothing I can truly call a memory.

The first real honest bit of light and shape did not come back into my life until the next day, or so I was told.

And to be truthful, I would have rather stayed in the dark.

The light was at a level 12 harshness, and the piercing shot of agony racing though my rib cage was a nasty reminder of the mountainside. The only good thing about my eye opening was the face greeting me.

It was blond, blue-eyed, and having trouble holding back the tears.

Not sure why.

I wasn't dead, at least not that I knew of.

While I questioned such a situation, Taylor finally worked up a half smile and coughed a short utterance in my direction, "I was so scared, Grandpa."

I tried forcing out an answer to assure my granddaughter, but doing so was just a daydream.

My throat felt locked in place tighter than the grip of the mountainside's boulder. Seeing my struggles, Taylor tried slipping in a few drops of water from the bedside water container.

A great idea, but I couldn't fight off the returning blackness long enough to swallow.

It was like that for the next couple of times I managed an eye opening. The only real change was the selection of faces hovering over me.

When my besieged relativity finally worked its way back to a normal waking, I was told that, for a couple of days, I had been in an extremely bad way.

I guess collapsing your lung on the side of a mountain is not a recommended activity for a guy my age.

Since I had missed everything shortly after my swan dive into the Witch Rose crack, I had a ton of questions, and I got four sets of answers. Two sets from the twins, and one each from Taylor and Loki, the pagan giant.

But nothing from Salem.

CHAPTER SIXTY-SIX

After listening to everyone tell me their independent version of the events, I put together a fairly accurate idea of what happened after my less-than-smart dive into the boulder crack.

For a long moment's hesitation, everyone semifroze. They exchanged glances and looked around the clearing, but that was all. No shouting or threatening or any other exchange. Even the old guy went slack-jawed.

Until my almost soundless scream broke the ice.

Taylor's first move was to go after me and tried to start her own slide down the crack. She might have made it, but Loki put a stop to that by latching on to her belt loop with one hand and trapping Taylor's body down against the rock with the other.

Taylor tried to angle herself for a trained kick at the giant pagan, but Loki's words put a stop to that as well.

"I'll hold your legs so you don't slide down and get caught as well."

While Loki and my granddaughter adjusted her entrance, Salem crossed to the other side of my slide position. Without giving anyone a chance to help or delay, Salem began edging down the crack feetfirst. She kept the feet spread and pushing again the up and down sides of the boulder. It gave Salem the leverage to hold off the uncontrolled slide I had used.

On the other side of the clearing, the opposition began making their movements as well.

The old man was throwing up his arms and urging his people forward. He towered over them like a raging Odin from his pagan past. Since his modern weapons would not work and ours were more powerful than his clubs and axes, the pagan switched over to an overwhelming force of numbers style of attack.

But that was not as easy as he hoped.

Jess's trident was mostly healed and stiff enough to inflict both slashing and stabbing damage. Jody was also getting the feel of her lance. Together they hedged to their left, placing themselves directly between my trapped body and their advances.

From the pagans' point of view, the twins must have looked like a pair of Amazon warriors who were after their hearts for lunch. It didn't help their courage to have already seen two of their force twinkle away to nothing.

Watching their less-than-eager advances, the girls were sure the oversize attackers would have gladly abandoned size advantage for working firearms. Hearing about it later, I could almost imagine their facial expressions caught between two fears.

But it took only seconds to choose between the two fears. Remembering the power of the old man behind them, three of them went toward Jess's off side with a flanking attack. Jess fizzled two of them away with a slash of her trident. Neither was hurt seriously by the cutting, but it didn't matter.

Again, it started as a bright multicolored sparkling around the wounds, only to spread through their bodies until they were nothing but a twinkling in the air.

The third of the three, who was missed by a whirl of Jess's trident blades, had no time to take advantage of her miss. Because as he stepped forward to do a delivery of his own killing blow with a small ax, he ran into Jody's extended lance as she stepped past her sister to cover Jess's back.

The blade of Jody's lance went through the pagan's naval and out the back two inches to the right of his spine like a ten-pound arrow. Another time and place, the force behind Jody's lunge would have likely gotten the blade stuck and twisted away with the man's fall to the ground.

But not this time. As the attacker fell away, his body sparkled away into the air and released the blade on its own.

Two of the other pagans got brave enough to come at Jody from the rear. They thought to take advantage of Jody's move to protect her sister, and it might have worked except the twins had acquired some new skills to go with their new weapons.

Feeling her sister's last move, Jess continued the spin in turn to cover her sister's back. The move didn't quite give her the angle for a full-powered attempt, but she did get an awkward stab off the front foot.

It was an easy dodge for the first of the two pagans. He leaned back hard into an ass-hugging dirt set down.

The second was not so lucky.

He twisted to the side and only got the merest of pinpricks.

Jess was the closest, and she's not even sure if the blow drew blood. But it did bring out a tiny flow of spark. It grew into a full-out sparkling, which was enough to bring forth the twinkling—and his doom.

CHAPTER SIXTY-SEVEN

Reaching down into the crack with Loki acting as an anchor, Taylor was able to get a grip on my calf just above the ankle. From her new position, she was able to see Salem out of the corner of her eye.

Salem was using her cat blood to get an awkward twist into her body, one that allowed her to get a hold on the other ankle.

Without waiting for Salem's aid, Taylor gave a grunting from deep in her gut's pull. As for results, Taylor couldn't be sure because of the heavy quivering in my leg.

There was a possible loosening coming at her through the fingertips but certainly no upward give.

Salem joined in with a pull of her own, but at best, she got nowhere you could measure. They each gave another pull on their own, when Loki put a stop to it with a cry from above.

"Do it together on the count of three!"

Taylor and Salem gave each other an understanding look, while above them, Loki shrieked out a "One!"

From there, Taylor wasn't sure if Loki huffed out his two, before or after Salem went into a spasmatic jerk, one so heavy it went beyond violent, shooting Salem out of her cramped-up body position into a spine-cracking, full-out stretch upward.

According to Taylor, Salem's explosion upward sucked me loose from the boulder with a snap, crackle, and pop of flesh and bone. It also had enough fierceness to snap my lower calf free of Taylor's grip and up past her shoulder. It was only her quick reaction that allowed her to reattach a grip well above my knee.

Behind Taylor, Loki shifted his offhand all the way up to Taylor's hip. He gathered it in resolutely and jerked both me and Taylor up another full foot and a half. Then with Taylor mostly free of the crack, he replaced her hold on my leg and dragged me the rest of the way out of the crack and onto the boulder's outer shelf.

Once Taylor was safe and I was free, Loki dropped to his knees and checked for a pulse and breathing. The first finding was unclear, while the second was a definite no go.

In response, Loki pushed his next inhale back out and into my lungs. After repeating the mouth-to-mouth a second time, he moved to give me chest compressions.

But Taylor shoved Loki's hand away.

"From the look of my grandfather's chest, there has to be some rib damage." Taylor held off his second attempt. "You might push a rib right through his heart or lungs."

Unsure for just a heartbeat of his own, Loki went back to forcing a third breath into my mouth. This time, the hesitation after the fourth such breath was for the big guy to take a check—a check that brought out a smile as my fifth breath came without his help.

With that, he stopped worrying about me and turned his attention to the war zone still in play.

CHAPTER SIXTY-EIGHT

The old man had his pagan attackers spread in a half circle around the girl, staying just out of reach of the twins' blades. From there, using multiple faints and dodges, they were hemming my girls back into a continually tightened area.

According to all concerned, it looked like, once penned into a small-enough area, the pagans would probably release a volley of clubs and axes.

Jess and Jody were both getting better at this old style of combat by the moment, but that was going to be an awful lot of thrown missiles for them to dodge.

"Enough!"

"You want to command now?"

"I want this over!"

The old pagan drew up to his fullest possible height and sent the look of Odin blasting toward his son. If the old man had been the real god, thunder and lightning bolts would have accompanied the glare.

"They destroyed the Witch Rose"—the dude went right past a simple god of the north to Moses on the mountainside—"and now they are going to die."

The men surrounding the twins were turning into bobble dolls, trying to take in both sides of the confrontation without missing anything. Most seemed to be under the spell of the elder pagan, nodding in agreement with his words but a few, with either the fresh memory of the recent twinkling away of their comrades riding the front of their mind or perhaps a growing sense of allegiances to the younger pagan's style of leadership.

Or maybe both.

These were the ones casting supportive glances in Loki's direction with everything he uttered.

"Not unless you want to die first."

From what appeared to be an extra deep back pocket, Loki drew out my Smith and Wesson .44 mountain revolver. He didn't exactly point it at his father, but it wasn't far-off.

But his dad was not one to be cowered by threats, even those uttered by his own son.

"Modern weapons do not work up here!"

Loki pointed my revolver skyward and eased it back and forth over head. You could see where he didn't actually have a finger on the trigger. Instead, he let it rest along the other edge of the barrel.

"Not while the Witch Rose was alive"—Loki made a show of folding his finger back to the trigger guard—"but the Witch Rose is gone."

With those words in the air, the old man lost an inch or so of tower. His next words were switched over to a different sense of questioning.

"I am your father."

"And I will grieve for you the rest of my life."

They held that way without speaking for over a minute.

Then a cloud seemed to build over the older pagan.

First of all, the skin resting over his cheekbones hardened into a black iron with the lips pressed into a thin line. And there was a burn in his eyes that his son had never seen before.

"Then I have no son."

That was the declaration that should have led to launching the attack, but it didn't. The old man broke off his towering stance. And once back to simple giant size, he waved for his people to follow him back down the mountainside.

Most did, but three held back, waiting for Loki's lead, which was lucky for me.

With the destruction of the Witch Rose, the cell phone began showing bars. It gave Jody a chance to get ahold of 911 and arrange a medevac to meet us on the highway.

But getting me there was another problem.

Again, the big guy stepped in.

With help from his remaining men and Jess, he put together a stretcher, while Jody took care of my medical needs. Carrying me to the cabins and then down on a circular route would have been the easiest path and the one to take with just the girls to do the lifting.

But with the presence of the pagans, Jody opted for a route at a ninety-degree angle from the cabins. It was a shorter and quicker way to the highway, but steeper, unknown, and much rougher terrain.

The three men who had stayed to help were not as big as Loki, but none of them had ever been called small or fragile, which was a good thing, because it took all their muscles and some added help from my twins and Taylor to keep my stretcher from sliding away out of control.

At least twice, one of the helpers went down with a twisted ankle, only to work themselves back up to continue helping my descent while doing their best to ignore the pain.

Finally, they reached the roadway just before the copter came into sight overhead. Then with some fancy arm waving and passing along information on the cell phone, my saviors got the copter down on the highway for my transit to the hospital, leaving all but Jody behind with three questions.

How were they going to get back to the trucks? The officers who had arrived to help with the copter landing were willing to take them into town. But they had other duties, so a trip back into the forest was out of the question. A call to those who had actually left with Loki's father got a better response. They were already approaching our abandoned trucks, and Loki was able to coax some volunteers to drive our trucks out to my rescuer's position. For good measure, a couple of others offered to provide their services to pick up Loki's three supporters. Apparently, Loki was the only one being disowned for his betrayal.

Question 2 was asked later, on the way to the hospital: would Loki have shot his father? The only answer the girls got from our giant friend was an honest one. Not even Loki was sure.

And the third and most important question: Where was Salem?

Chapter Sixty-Nine

Taking the story back to the mountainside clearing, Taylor remembered seeing Salem on the far side of my body when I popped out.

Salem didn't seem to be doing much moving as a person, but there was the jerking around of a changeover.

Taylor didn't think it was going right.

It was too slow and seemed to be hitting Salem in a scattergun method, with first an arm showing silver fur and then smoothing out to human pink. Then the leg shortened up into the size of her feline persona, only to snap out to its normal length an eye flick later. Even Salem's face simmered out of focus, only to snap back with every feature crystal clear like a high-definition television.

Thinking back to the sight later, Taylor thought it was almost like the changeover to a cat was being forced against Salem's will. And she thought Salem's eyes were full of an unbearable agony.

But then Taylor had to bring her attention back to me, to halt Loki's attempted compressions to the chest. By the time Loki had reinflated my lungs and dragged me back to the living, Taylor's return look found nothing.

None of the others had seen even that much.

The twins cursed themselves for not checking around better, but getting me down to the highway seemed more important at the moment. It wasn't until the next day had passed that anyone got back up the mountainside.

Loki and his followers found nothing.

After my first short visit with Taylor, Loki tried a second time with Taylor and Jess joining in. They had no better luck and could only believe some creature had dragged her away as a cat, or more likely, Salem had drifted off into the nether regions following after the Witch Rose.

I wanted to throw a temper tantrum, but I couldn't blame them for leaving Salem behind.

I myself had just been forced into making the right choice over the wanted choice just moments before theirs. I knew in my heart, saving the lives of who knows how many children had to be the right way to go.

But at the same time, that was a future we might have found another way around.

Destroying Salem?

That was a right-now move with no chance for a later do-over.

So now, I was hating myself for it.

For the second time in my life, I hurt so bad inside there didn't seem much reason for going on.

Chapter Seventy

I know I would have eventually snapped out of it.

After all, I had two daughters and a granddaughter who depended on me. I owed it to them to keep on living in the best manner possible.

But the nightmare never gave me the chance to do so.

It came into my room the night before I was supposed to go home to Michigan.

Jody had already taken Taylor back to Hemlock.

My granddaughter needed to be in Michigan for the start of school. And after I had been moved to a regular room and there wasn't much reason for them to hang around and watch me heal.

Jess had stayed behind to watch over me in case any problems arose. But even she didn't stay at my bedside all the time.

Tonight, Jess had stopped in early and then gone back to her room at the end of visiting hours. She planned on packing up our ride and returning to the hospital the next morning right before dismissal time.

With the end of visiting hour, the only ones left on the floor were the night nurses, and they were getting pretty good at letting me sleep. They had not woken me up to give me a sleeping pill in over a week.

Still, for some unknown reason, I woke up.

It wasn't from a noise.

True, there were night noises around, the ones you always heard in the ward—you know, a chattering hum from the nurse's station and the clattering of med carts making their rounds. But not much of anything out of place.

Still, I had a sense something was different.

I tried holding my breath and checking out all the corners of the room.

There was nothing.

Just a few shadows deeper than the rest, and not much of a danger.

And then a huge form detached itself from the window-side shadow and misted over to the end of my bed.

And in response, my heart froze to a stop.

I thought of forcing a scream out but knew I would be dead before the nurses could get here. And I had to believe the old man would either be gone or, worse, go through the nurses with the force of a bulldozer changing them over from caregivers to patients.

My body was still hurting, but I wasn't going to make it easy on the old pagan. If he wanted to finish our confrontation from the mountainside, he was going to pay a price himself.

But he didn't move up from the foot of the bed.

The old man just hovered there, like a specter from my worst nightmare.

It didn't help my status that the giant had brought a couple of weapons along as well.

He had a cloth bundle tucked under one arm, probably to cover my face while slicing my neck with the metal piece he held in his other hand.

"You survived."

I caught enough reflective gleam in the old pagan's eyes to confuse me. It didn't look like hate or anything I could pin a name on.

"Loki said you would."

That made me wonder if father and son were back to talking, but only for a moment before fear chased that away.

The old man leaned toward me to bring his piece of metal into play, but again I choked off the effort to sit up as the object came into focus.

It wasn't a blade or even anything sharp.

What the pagan held out to me had the form and shape of a detective badge without the holder.

I swallowed hard and forced out a whisper, "Green-Jeans?"

"Loki never trusted him."

I nodded an understanding.

"I hoped his fear of me would make him choose a side." The old man lowered retired detective Green-Jeans's badge down to my bed, where he left it nestled between my feet.

Once free of the badge, Loki's father straightened up and then used his free hand to retuck the bundle under his other arm for a better hold.

"He didn't."

I rolled around several words of my own but never got any of them uttered. I was beginning to think I did not want to know any more about Green-Jeans's story.

"He hurt innocent people."

I gave a nod, thinking about the cabin people and, to a personal degree, my granddaughter and her innocence. I could see where Taylor might never forget the pulling of the trigger that sent a body tumbling to hell.

"He escaped our ambush of the Arabs."

"And now?"

"I found him, and he paid for his sins against me and mine."

Again, the pagan master shifted his bundle for a better grip. I tried hard but could not put a name to the shape and size of the package. I could only image the old man had it brought along to help with my end.

"My turn?"

The old man's look alone was enough to peel away my skin and was leaving me with a feeling beyond naked. I was almost at the point where my doom would be an upgrade.

"It's your time for an equaling." I watched the old man shift his bundle out from under his arm and into a double handhold to bring it out toward me. "But not one of vengeance."

Chapter Seventy-One

Igulped down his last words like a diamond drops of grace. For the first time since his appearance, the icy chill left my spine and I felt like I might see my kids at least once more.

"Then why?"

The pagan lowered the bundle down to my bed, but without releasing the tucks of the material.

Then his eyes meant mine.

"My son Loki reminded me you fought your battle to help people." The pagan's look hardened as if he was regretting something, either the words he was about to say about something or a past action. "Unlike the rest of us."

He hesitated for a very long thought before giving a pat to the bundle before he continued, "And since I have already lost his older brother Thor to my unbending beliefs, I do not want to do the same with Loki."

Another story I was never going to hear?

But I had to know something, even if I didn't get the full story. "Are you Odin?"

"No, my given name is Hans."

The following shake of his head was somewhere between sad and possible relief. "My son's naming came more from the influence of my father than my mother."

"Loki?"

That didn't seem as man controlled as Thor.

"Not my father's or my first choice of names."

I was finding it hard to believe the god of the mountainside had a softer side. This talk was becoming like water running back up the Niagara Falls.

"Loki was my wife's little joke." Another backstory I was never going to know.

"Enough family knowledge." The big guy's hand cut through the air like a war ax. "I brought you this as an offering. I found it in the brush further down the boulder when I went back to check on the Witch Rose."

Great! Just what I needed. A reminder of the cost of my decision back in the clearing. Wasn't it bad enough the pain still tugged on my soul like an out-of-control passenger train?

Hans, the ancient pagan, began an untucking of the bundle with his left hand, while I tried to work up the energy for a rejection.

Whatever it was, I didn't want it.

At least not until I caught a glint of color.

I couldn't be sure in the dimness of my room, but I thought it had the look of tarnished silver. Not the shine of the silver I was looking for, but awful close to the hue I had dreamed about these hours before.

Only it couldn't be.

That one stretched out to a silken strand with a living sheen to it.

Then the old man pulled back some more of the cotton wrapping to show me more of the subject matter. It definitely looked organic, and I knew I shouldn't, but I began to hope.

I found myself sitting up and leaning forward into the final opening of the bundle. And as the rest of my pagan's offering came into sight, with it my world quivered.

She didn't look good with her tarnished silver hair being more wire than silk, but I knew who she was.

"Salem?"

That got me a head raise and half mew.

Then with a weakened effort, Salem dragged herself a few steps to curl up against my side just above the hip. Once there, she went into a purr, not exactly a feline one, but a purr all of Salem's own.

"I think she'll heal." The pagan almost reached out to pet or pat the cat at my side but hesitated to a halt at the last moment. "She already looks better than when I found her."

"Can she?"

"Not now, maybe never." Again, his hand twitched a bit in Salem's direction. "But at best, it will take time for your cat lady to be able to choose her shape at will."

I brought my own hand down to clasp Salem into my side. There was more of my heat going into her than living comfort coming into mine.

But I was glad to give it.

After a moment, I lifted my head back to the pagan to tell him thank you.

But he wasn't there. Even the badge and the material of the bundle were gone.

I checked the shadows, but even though they were darker than black now, I could tell they were empty.

I whispered a thank-you into the air and settled back to wait for the morning sun to come up.

That should have been the end of it all, but what did I know?

CHAPTER SEVENTY-TWO

My room was flooded even before the beginning of visiting hours. Not only did Jess show up to take me home, but both Taylor and Jody had come back from Michigan to help her. And to really fill up the room, Loki had come along to aid them as well.

It was like a large flock of geese in a very small field.

But I was the center of attention for less than a minute.

As Jody moved into a hug, it pulled my untucked sheet free from my side. Doing so exposed Salem, and it didn't take a pulsebeat for Taylor to bump her aunt to one side. She went into a bend-over hug, which sprayed tears on to the fur of her childhood friend.

Maybe with less tears, but deepened visual emotions showing all the same, the twins crowded around to give Salem some gentle strokes and human "awws."

It was Loki who kept his attention focused on me. He moved around to the other side of my bed and mouthed a "My father?"

"Last night."

Jess caught enough of our back-and-forth out of the corner of her eye to get the gist of it. And she backed away from Salem to take a detailed survey of the room.

It took Jess the better part of five minutes. Only then did she ask her question.

"Did your father bring the flowers as well?"

"Does my father seem the type to bring flowers?"

"Your father doesn't seem the type to bring Salem back to us." Jess looked back at my bedside and completed the answer with a tilted head. "At least not while she was still breathing."

"My father is a man of rigid beliefs." Loki stepped over toward the flowers Jess had mentioned. "But back in our home country, he is also known for having a kind heart to his friends and family."

"But not for people like retired detective Green-Jeans."

At the mention of the detective's name, Loki gave me the coldest grin I had ever perceived on a human face. It was only as he gathered up the flowers to bring over to my bedside that it faded back toward his friendlier face. Only after he settled the flowers down where we all could study them did the smile appear normal again.

"Unfortunately for Green-Jeans, my father never forgives the morally challenged." Loki put his hand over mine. "But with perhaps just a few gentle nudges from me, my father realized you were a foe who deserved to be treated as an honorable equal."

I put my other hand over Loki's but still fell short of encircling his single fist. "Thank you, I'm glad his son is such a farsighted being."

"What about the flowers?"

Jess reached over Salem to finger the plant on my eating tray and spread it a bit for all to see.

It was a vine-like plant with red buds not yet in blossom. To my recollection, I had never seen such a plant, yet for some reason, they looked familiar. It wasn't anything I had ever grown or seen in a neighbor's garden.

"They weren't here last night when I left you."

"Or when I woke up this morning to take a nurse-aided shower." Taylor gave out a huff at the word *shower* and didn't seem to care for me taking such a shower. So for her sake and maybe a better chance to tease my granddaughter, I added, "Before becoming a nurse, he was an all-star high school football player with a damaged knee, and he was only with me to prevent any falling."

That put a damper on Taylor's teenage outrage well before it got to full-out offended mode. To make the point even further, said nurse chose that moment to come into my room.

He was pushing a hospital wheelchair, which was needed for my release, and perhaps a little surprised at the size of the gathering in my room.

"Hey, Robert"—not sure if it should have been *Robert* or *Bob*, but either way, I figured it was better than "Hey, you"—"do you know who delivered the flowers?"

"No one. We have been busy and haven't gotten around to delivering anything yet."

We exchanged looks all around, while the nurse gave us an "Are you crazy?" look before carefully placing the chair by the wall and disappearing out the door.

"It looks familiar."

I nodded.

Taylor gave out a short look to the ceiling and then solved the mystery. "Spread the biggest bud out."

When we didn't react quickly enough, my granddaughter took matters in her own hands. She went around the end of the bed to push Loki aside and take over with the flower.

With a strong but gentle touch, Taylor used two fingers and her thumb to fold down the petals. As we had seen from across the room by looking at the buds, the flower was a deep red with a white trim around the outer edge. An exact opposite of the flowers of our Witch Rose.

"You have got to be kidding."

Not 100 percent sure, but I think I was the one to make the utterance. For a moment, both Loki and I were beyond stunned while it was taking a bit longer for it to sink in for the twins. After all, they had never actually seen a Witch Rose in bloom.

Only Taylor showed no surprise.

While we remained in shock, Taylor marched over to the side-bar where the flowers had been sitting. It took her only a second to come up with a card that had been stuck in place by the moisture of the vase.

She waved it semidry and then opened it with all the drama of a Shakespeare ending. And then with a loss of color none of us had expected, she read the words.

I held out my hand for the card but got a verbal reading instead.

"Not all Witch Roses are evil."

About the Author

C. T. Heinlein was born in Bay City, Michigan, and was part of the second graduation class of Bay City's John Glenn High School.

After dropping out of the Air Force Academy, he attended Central Michigan University in Mount Pleasant, Michigan, where he earned a BS in education.

A wrestler in high school, he went on to do judo in college. After graduation, Heinlein used his love of sports to teach and coach a number of different sports in Kuwait, Liberia, and upon his return to the States, Texas and Michigan.

As a father of two and grandfather of four, he learned the true meaning of "If you are close enough to be a friend, you're close enough to be considered family." Now his family includes onetime students, many friends of his kids, and a collection of the best people this world has to offer.

This extended family helps him survive the loss of his son Charlie Junior in Iraq and gives him the strength to keep writing and dreaming.

CPSIA information can be obtained
at www.ICGtesting.com
Printed in the USA
BVHW040532120523
663884BV00001B/1

9 781662 461576